Three Mods
Tony Barrett

The events leading up and including the August Bank Holiday weekend of 1964, The Second Battle of Hastings as seen through the eyes of three young Mods, whose stories although separate, all describe that eventful weekend, which will change their lives and bring them together.

Originally available on Kindle, the stories are now combined in this paperback edition.

August '64 Extended

The Summer Of '64

Bird's Eye View

Acknowledgements:

Many thanks to Mick Stewart who goes through my work with a fine toothcomb, spotting all the errors I have missed and pushed me onto write the final part of the trilogy.

Also, Paul and Chrissy Stubley to ensure the story hung together and for their encouragement, and to ensure I got the Rocker side of the story correct.

And a big thank you to Erin Starr over there on island of Maui, Hawaii for taking the trouble to get her head around some very non-American spelling and expressions, one reason for the addition of a glossary at the end of the book.

Cover Design: 'Clacton 1964' with kind permission of the artist Andy Crabb.

Dedication:

This book is dedicated to my late wife Linda Barrett, a real 1960's Mod girl who died tragically earlier this year, 2018.

I did not meet her until 1967, three years after the events of 1964, but she had that 'Mod Spirit' all through her life and was a wonderful wife and caring mother to our children Emma and Ben.

ISBN: 9781977059314

Contents:

August '64 (Steve's Story)

In 1964 gangs of Mods and Rockers fought battles on the very British beaches Winston Churchill had once sworn to defend.

Clacton at Easter and Margate at Whitsun had seen the seaside towns invaded by the scooter and motorcycle youngsters.

Now the August Bank Holiday was drawing near and Mods like Steve in Southend on Sea waited to find out which coastal town would be next.

5-4-3-2-1 – Manfred Mann

Steve was feeling pretty well chuffed, he had passed his motor cycle driving test and could finally dispense with his L plates, and could now carry pillion passengers legally which was just as well as the Easter Bank Holiday was just days away and if all the rumours were correct it looked like they were all heading for Clacton.

Tearing the L plates in half and dumping them in the waste bin at the testing centre in Southend on Sea he set off home, a wide grin on his face as his gunned the Vespa 125 into the traffic.

Over the last few days all the talk had been about the upcoming weekend and the planned excursion to the Essex seaside town.

It was traditional for Londoners to get away from the Smoke for the Bank Holiday breaks, Clacton a favourite for East Londoners and Brighton, Margate and Hastings for those who lived in the south of the city, but the weather for the weekend did not look promising.

"So, who you takin'? Bandy Malc asked.

"Smudger."

"Wot that bird who works in Boots the Chemist in the High Street?"

"Yeah, only problem is she's gotta work all day on Saturday."

"So, you gonna get over to Clacton Saturday night?"

"Sunday probably." Steve replied.

"Think Easter Monday is when most of the stuff is going on, loads of Mods from all over coming to Clacton, like a gigantic meeting of the Mod clan, should be fun."

"The weather forecast looks like the weather is gonna be shitty, fucking typical Bank Holiday weather."

"It's bloody Easter, you ain't gonna be laying on the beach sunbathing or going swimming." Bandy Malc reminded Steve.

"Where you gonna stay?"

"Dunno, gonna take me sleeping bag just in case."

"Do I know her?"

"Fucking comedian."

Later that evening Steve's oldest friend came around to see him, the roar of his BSA announcing his arrival before he got to the front door.

Steve opened the door and watched Fred walk up the path dressed in his leathers and silk scarf wrapped around his face, his crash helmet in his hand.

"Bloody freezing tonight, thought I saw a brass monkey down on the corner looking for his balls." Fred laughed.

"Passed me test." Boasted Steve.

"About time, thought those L plates were a permanent feature on that old rust bucket of yours."

"You only passed your test a couple of weeks ago." Remonstrated Steve.

"What's this shit I'm hearing about the weekend?"

"What Clacton?"

"Yeah. You know it's not only Mods going, don't you? Rockers have been going to Clacton for the Bank Holiday for years and that adds up to trouble."

"What, fighting?"

"Why should there be trouble, here in Southend the Mods and Rockers tolerate each other without any bother, yeah the odd scuffle here and there but generally nothing serious."

"I just got a gut feeling. Those East London Mods have been giving grief to the Rockers up there and that don't bode well." Fred said.

"Are you going?" Steve asked.

"Yeah, half a dozen of us on Easter Monday, but we ain't looking for any aggro."

"Well stay out of trouble." Steve added.

Steve stood huddled in the doorway across the High Street from Boots the Chemist waiting for Sue Smith or 'Smudger' as she had got herself nicknamed at school for the state of her exercise books, to finish work. It was freezing and Steve had his parka wrapped around him, his hands deep in the pockets, hood pulled up but the chilled wind was still cutting right through him.

Just after six o'clock Steve spotted Sue coming out of the side entrance and walked across the road to meet her.

"Hello darlin', fancy a lift home?"

"You passed your test?" Sue said with a big smile on her face.

"Yep, and now I can take you to Clacton."

"Well I hope it fucking well warms up a bit."

"At least it ain't raining." Said Steve trying to be positive.

"Come on, I'll give you a lift home rather than you standing about waiting for a bus."

"Look I got something today, an uncollected prescription for Drinamyl so I half-hitched it. Must be sixty tablets in the little tablet bottle. Enough to keep us going for a bit, Eh?"

"You gotta be careful, if they catch you nicking tablets you will be in deep shit."

"This one had been on the collections shelf for ages, no-one saw me and it seemed such a shame to see them going to waste."

"They certainly won't be wasted now." Said Steve with a grin on his face.

"Come on girl let's get moving before we freeze to death."

That Girl Belongs To Yesterday- Gene Pitney

If Steve thought the weather could not get any worse he was in for a big surprise, driving rain and freezing winds made the drive up to Chelmsford, then Colchester before following the Clacton signs had been a nightmare. Sue had moaned most of the way and when they were turned away from numerous bed and breakfast hotels or noticed the 'No Vacancy' signs in the windows, they had resulted into breaking into a beach hut for shelter from the elements.

They had met up with Bandy Malc, Big Ron, Mike Smith and Marshy under the pier but as high tide was later that evening they had to find alternative sleeping arrangements. The beach huts were suggested by a local Mod who felt sorry for their plight, looking bedraggled, wet and cold.

They had tried a bonfire on the beach with deck-chairs but it was a losing battle, and had resulted in sharing out the purple hearts to lift their spirits.

The beach hut was only just big enough for the group and Sue being the only girl soon made it very clear she was far from happy at being cooped up with five far from fresh unwashed damp Mods.

About a thousand Mods had arrived in the town and every doorway was crowded with dispirited and damp Mods. The town was dead out of season, nothing much was open and even the pubs had closed at 2 O'clock. Boredom was becoming rampant.

Easter Monday morning saw little respite from the weather and as the crowds of Mods assembled in the town with nothing to do it was only a matter of time before something sparked off trouble and that something was the heavy-handed approach of the local police.

Suddenly the mood changed to anger and as if one the pier became the object of their frustration, the Mods pissed off and not willing to pay the one shilling entrance fee stormed the pier, jumping over the turnstiles and invading the structure. Windows were broken and a bit of damage was incurred.

The police moved in and started arresting Mods, who now turned their attention on a group of Rockers who were witnessing the whole affair from the promenade and a chase through the streets developed. In reality there was no more violence than at any football match on a normal Saturday in Southend but the sight of hundreds of Mods caused panic among the holiday makers, encouraging the police to become ever more aggressive in their actions.

During the charge on the pier Steve had lost sight of Sue and now was desperately trying to find her.

"Think I saw her over by the jellied eel shop being chatted up by that Ace Face from Romford." Said Mike.

"Did you see where she went?" Demanded Steve.

"I think I saw her get in his car." Mike said sheepishly.

"So, did you do anything about it?" Steve said angrily.

"What could I do? Those Romford Mods are hard cases and as far as I could see she wasn't objecting to the offer."

"Fucking cow, she has been fucking moaning the whole fucking weekend about being cold, wet and bored. Wished I had never have brought her."

"Better off without her." added Big Ron Nicholson.

"I have enough of the shit hole, let's get back to civilisation, and one thing I have fucking learnt is travel fucking light, leave the bloody girls at home."

"I would drink to that if the fucking pubs were open." Said Mike with more than a hint of resignation in his voice.

"Wild Ones Invade Seaside- 97 Arrests, scooter gangs beat up Clacton," said Steve's father as he prodded the front page of the Daily Mirror, "Bloody hooligans that's what I call you lot."

Steve just stood there trying to keep his cool.

"Bring back National Service, that's what the government should do. Bloody tearaways ruining people's lives."

"The whole thing has been blown out of all proportion, nothing much happened." Steve said defensively.

"Are you saying the newspapers lie?"

"Yes, I was there and there was a bit of trouble but nothing like the bloody papers are making it out to be."

"And you expect me to believe you when I have the evidence here in front of me in black and white?"

"What evidence?"

"97 arrests, that sounds like a whole heap of evidence to me."

"Well no-one I know was arrested."

"Well I am bloody pleased to hear that because if you were arrested you would certainly have upset your mother and me."

Bits and Pieces-The Dave Clark Five

It was nearly three thirty in the morning when Steve pushed his dead Vespa up the drive of his parent's house and put it into the garden shed. Normally he would have wiped it down, but tonight or rather this morning he felt like giving it a quick kicking. It had died after he had dropped off his girlfriend or to be more accurate his former girlfriend and he had pushed the bike for as near damn it nearly three miles back to his home. His white parallels were mud spattered and dirty, he was sweating through exertion and the lingering effects of the uppers he had taken earlier, but were now wearing off adding to his pissed off disposition.

A group of Rockers riding past him pushing the Vespa had not helped his already bad temper. Apart from a number of lurid comments they had not stopped, but he recognised one the motorbikes as a BSA Gold Star, the mount of his friend but because he was a Rocker and Steve a Mod it had not been possible for him to have stopped and help.

Now more determined more than ever to get himself a new scooter on the never-never to replace his clapped out one two five, with a later model, and not the embarrassing machine he had at the moment. It had served him to pass his driving test, but now the speedo did not work, and it was becoming two-tone, green and rust, and not worth spending too much more money on to keep it going.

His date that night like his scooter had come to an abrupt halt, Sandra Dee had been giving him the come on but when it came to it she like the Vespa had shut down and was having none of it.

Feeling the onset of the downer that followed the hearts he had taken earlier, he quietly went in the back door and into his bedroom.

With the August Bank Holiday on the horizon, he would need to get some finances together to put down a deposit on a new or nearly new Vespa Sportique 125. He would have really liked a Vespa GS 160 but that was just out of his price range. It was the dog's bollocks and the scooter that all the faces were riding but he would have to get the best he could afford.

His mate Bandy Malc had a Lambretta LI 150 which was faster than his current scooter, but at the moment everything was faster than his current wheels.

Lambretta's had the reputation of being generally faster than the Vespa but had reliability problems as the drive shafts couldn't take the punishment being dished out by over enthusiastic acceleration and that he could do without.

Now alone in his room, unable to sleep, Steve tried to take account of himself and was disappointed at the result: No girlfriend, dead end job with no prospects, scooter broke and he was trying hard to think of something positive. He was a number not a ticket, had some good gear including a new three-button two-piece suit with side vents, Fred Perry shirts and wasn't that bad looking or at least that was what he told himself, and he had a few bob in his pocket.

If he could get his 'A' level art GCE he would be able to get out of his mundane job he was in now, although when chatting up birds telling them he was in the picture business sounded cool, in reality it was making picture frames in a little factory in Rochford, which was not so glamourous.

With an 'A' level he could go to art school and try and get into advertising which was what he really wanted to do.

When sleep finally came it was a welcome relief from the real world.

In his dreams he sat astride a Vespa GS 160, ten mirrors, two spot lamps, leather covered backrest, chromed bubbles, a real Ace Face with little adoring Mod girls all around him all desperately trying to get his attention as he pretended not to notice, as he was waiting for the queen of the Mods Cathy McGowan to try and tempt him off his scooter and dance with her as the music increased in intensity. She reached out her hand to touch his face and beckon him towards her, her intention full of promise.

He watched Cathy's smile, her lips inviting as she called him.

"Come on. Come on." The voice called cutting through the music.

"Come on wake up you lazy little sod. It's time you got up for work."

Slowly he opened his red rimmed eyes, lack of sleep and the after-effects of the uppers, as he mother shook him back to sensibility.

"You look terrible Stevie." His mum said with some concern.

"Me scooter conked out and I had to push it home."

"Come and have some breakfast and a cup of coffee and I am sure you will feel better, it's all ready for you."

Steve groaned, and thought a couple of Purple Hearts would do him a lot more good than a couple of bits of toast and a cup of Camp coffee.

A Hard Day's Night- The Beatles

Steve heard the roar of the Beeza coming up the road before the motorbike arrived and stopped outside of his parent's house. On the ground in front of him was a pile of parts from his scooter which he was desperately trying to put back together before it rained.
"Having fun?" said Fred as he removed his helmet.
"Does it fucking well look like I'm having fun?" groaned Steve as he lit another ciggie.
Fred looked at the pile of bits and smiled to himself, "Clutch go again."
"Yep. Had to push the fucking thing back home last night."
"Thought you might have been doing a bit of late night exercise when I saw you last night, but there was no way I could stop to help you. Well if you will ride a fucking souped-up hair dryer rather than a real motorbike so what do you expect?"
Steve looked towards Fred's BSA Gold Star stood by the gate and then back at his partially dismantled Vespa, "Hardly go down that well if I turned up on one of those, would it?"
"I suppose a Goldie would not be the right image for a Mod, would it?"
Fred knelt down and started to sort out the parts and started to reassemble the clutch, the idea of a Rocker rebuilding a Mod's scooter would probably not really have gone down that well with his mates, but he and Steve went back a long way. They had been at primary school together, then secondary school and both learnt to ride motorbikes at the same time, but Steve had cut his hair, ditched the Brylcreem and followed the modernist trend.
"At least the Vespa is easy to start, doesn't break your fucking ankle to kick-start it and is more civilised." Said Steve.
"Yeah, but with 500cc it is faster than your 125 and a load of fun to ride you are never going to get a ton-up down the Southend Arterial on this are you?"
"You know we are never going to agree, don't you?
"You stick to your black leathers and grease, and I'll keep my parka."
With surprising ease Fred soon had the Vespa back together and to Steve's evident relief it stated at the first attempt.
"So, what's new?" Fred asked.
"Not much, still at the picture framing factory, making a few bob but still going to evening school for my 'A' levels down at Southend College."
"I got an interview with IBM in London next week repairing electric typewriters." Said Fred.
"What about your job at the garage?" Steve inquired.
"Ain't going nowhere, pissed off with pumping gas to arseholes."
"No more free petrol."
"Well don't turn up at your interview in your leathers, you need to make a good impression. You can borrow me new suit if you want?"
"Nah it's OK me mum bought me some new clobber to wear."
"You still going out with that bird Jenny from the newsagents?" Steve asked.
"Yeah any port in a storm if you know what I mean?" smirked Fred.

"Well she ain't known as the village bicycle for nothing. Didn't know she liked greasers though."

"You've never been out with her, have you?"

"No but I went out with her sister, when she worked in the chemist, used to get me a few purple hearts and black bombers."

The sudden slam of the gate alerted Fred and Steve to the arrival of Bandy Malc who lived a just few doors down the road, "Thought I heard you arrive an hour or so ago up to no good I suspect."

"Jinx here thought he would strip down his scooter, without taking a note of where the bits went. Typical."

"I just got my side panels chromed, looks real neat." Boasted Bandy Malc.

"Shame it doesn't make it go any faster." Joked Fred.

"It's for effect to help pull the birds something you rockers would not understand." Malc said without malice.

"Being a Rocker is about speed, making sure your machine is in tip-top condition, the thrill of opening it up on an empty road with your mates," Fred looked at his watch before reaching for his bone-dome, "Time I was coloured gone and let you decide what you are going to wear or whatever is you Mods chat about. See you around."

Steve and Malc watched as Fred kicked his Beesa into life, the throaty roar 500cc engine echoing down the empty road.

"So, are you going into Southend tonight?"

"Dunno. Ain't got much cash. Might have to go into Rayleigh and do the old soda syphon scam." Admitted Steve.

"One day they are gonna catch you going over the fence nicking soda syphons from that shed out the back of the pub and then taking them in to the bar to collect the cash for them."

"Get seven shillings and sixpence for each one, easy cash." Boasted Steve.

"OK. See you down the Harold Dog on Saturday."

No Particular Place To Go- Chuck Berry

"How long you gonna be in there?" Shouted Steve's old man.

"Dunno, about another half hour I reckon," Steve said as he looked down into the bathwater wondering just how long it would take to shrink his new Levi jeans that cost him four pounds ten shillings.

"Jesus Christ what the hell are you doing in there?"

"Getting me new jeans to fit proper."

"Now I have heard everything. Take my word that you won't be wearing jeans when you are my age."

Steve raised two fingers at the closed door, reached for his packet of Guards and took one out and lit it.

It had been a shitty week and wasn't getting any better. The bastards had put up coils of barbed wire over the back fence of the pub in Rayleigh severely curtailing that avenue of finance.

His job rubbing down picture frames was hardly the stuff of dreams, but it was a job and if he was honest he was jealous of Fred getting an interview with IBM and working in London. There had to be something else he could do. He was good at art and had the 'O' level to prove it, but as his dad had said "There ain't no money in painting pictures." And had stopped him taking the entrance exam to the London College of Commercial Art.

Fred had always been good with his hands, taking stuff apart and usually putting them back together in working order.

It had been Fred who had found him his first motorbike and had talked Steve into buying a clapped out BSA Bantam, 4bhp with a suggested top speed of forty-five miles per hour, which as it turned out proved to be wildly optimistic. The whole thing including the wheel rims were painted in a mist-green which only highlighted the red-brown rust patches.

"It's a good little runner." Fred had said, but as it turned out the only running was pushing the bloody thing when it conked out.

"You've brought what?" Fred had questioned as he clapped eyes on Steve's first scooter, "A bloody Vespa?"

"Well it's faster than that bloody Bantam, still only a 125 but it goes."

"At least it is the same colour as the Bantam, a sort of a milky bile green." Fred joked, you'll be cutting your hair next.".

"Already have, the barber down on the Broad Parade did me a Beatle cut."

"What did he use a pudding basin?"

"Very funny, it's all the trend now you know. No more Brylcreem."

"Jesus, you are turning into one of them Modernists." Fred declared.

"It's what gets the birds these days."

"Those Mod girls look more like blokes with their short hair."

"You're just getting picky in your old age."

"So, you won't be going up to the Blinkin' Owl tonight?"

"No."

Although their paths parted Steve and Fred kept very much in touch, the fact that they followed different tribes would not affect their friendship, except when they were out when they would studiously ignore each other. It was not good for your street-cred to be seen in the company of a Rocker.

When Steve had sold on his tatty 125 onto his friend Mike, and brought his second-hand 1962 red Vespa Sportique 125, he was pretty damned chuffed, a down deposit and the rest on the old never-never it looked like new. Now fitted out with half a dozen Stadium wing mirrors and a rear seat rest it was beginning to look real cool.
Fred had given his new Vespa Sportique the once over.
"Still only a 125cc." Fred noted.
"Couldn't afford the 150 or a 175 and speed ain't everything."
"The whole essence of a motorbike is to be able to do a ton-up on the Southend Arterial. That feeling of the wind in yer face and the power between your legs. That's what life is all about."
"That's the difference, with a scooter you get to go between some bird's legs."
"Is that what all Mod's think about?" Fred demanded.
Steve laughed, "Well apart from keeping up with the latest clothes trends and the best R&B and Ska sounds, yes I suppose it is."
"That's alright then, a bird on the back of yer bike gets turned on by speed, so I suppose we ain't that much different after all."

World Without Love-Peter and Gordon

It was just like every other Saturday night for Steve, not much money left after being paid and after having to give his mum thirty shillings for bed and board out of his wages. He was between birds and it looked like his luck was not going to change tonight even the poker dice were not going his way.

"Come on roll the dice." Demanded Bandy Malc.

Steve picked up the remaining two dice, prayed for two jacks and rolled the dice across the Formica table top, and got fuck all.

"That makes ten games to me, four aces beat three jacks." Malc gloated with a big smile across his face.

"Ain't my night." Bemoaned Steve watching the two girls at the next table, one of which he really fancied but were getting chatted up by his friends John Marsh known usually as 'Marshy' and Mike Smith.

"Wanna play again?" Bandy Malc asked.

"Gotta be more to a Saturday night than playing Poker Dice."

"Could go down the bowling alley on the pier if it ain't burnt down again."

"Bit skint this week, had to buy a new button-down Ben Sherman shirt this week from Harry Fenton's in Rayleigh and the parts for me scooter."

Down the stairs into the basement the arrival of Big Ron Nicholson caught Steve's eye and he waved him over.

"You heard the latest? The word has filtered down from the Smoke that Hastings is on for the August Bank Holiday next weekend."

Bandy Malc stood up and shouted over Green Onions by Booker T and the MG's blasting away on the juke box, "Now pin back your lug holes and take note, it's 'astings next weekend, so get your glad rags ready we are going to the seaside."

"Make a change from Clacton and Margate." Said Mike Smith.

"Thought it might be Brighton this time." Bandy Malc

"At least the weather was better at Whitsun." Steve added, "And for the first time we really outnumbered the Rockers."

"Sawdust Caesars, that fucking judge in Margate called us, when he banged up a load of Mods." Mike said.

"These long-haired, mentally unstable, petty little hoodlums, these 'Sawdust Caesars' who can only find courage, like rats, in hunting in packs, came to Margate with the avowed intent of interfering with the life and property of its inhabitants." Steve added quoting the judge in a stern judicial voice.

"Long hair was out of style in May so he must have been referring to the Rockers." Laughed Mike.

"Had more grief from the South London Mods than we did from the Rockers, the North London Mods hated South London Mods. South London Mods hated North London Mods, and East London Mods hated everybody, and everybody hated them." Steve added.

"Problem was we outnumbered the Rockers I reckon by ten to one." Bandy Malc said summing up the situation.

"Got a couple of the South London Mods on the beach during that fucking football match, one tried to play the off-side rule so I whacked him with a deckchair. Taught them bastards not to under-estimate us Southend Mods."

Stated Big Ron with a smile on his face.

"My ole man went fucking mad at me when he saw that fucking Daily Mirror headline, 'Wild Ones Invade Seaside', especially after the Clacton and gave me a whole load of grief, calling me a hooligan." Admitted Steve

"I got a quid from a photographer who set up a frame of three of us Mods setting about a Rocker who afterwards was right pissed off as he only got ten bob." Mike boasted.

"The fucking press were there stirring up the shit looking to make it out to be full out fucking war between us and the Rockers. Yes, there was a bit of chasing, few bruises and cuts but that mostly happened on the beach playing football, but that was just between the Mods."

"Must admit I didn't see much agro either." Agreed Steve.

"Weren't there a battle at Hastings?" Marshy asked.

"Didn't you do history at school?" Mike demanded.

"'O' level in Social and Economic History but I don't remember a mention of a Battle at Hastings." Marshy answered.

"Bet you thought Arkwrights Spinning Jenny was some kind of acrobatic twirling bint." Bandy Malc chirped in.

"That's what going to Grammar School gets you." Steve added, "That head on his shoulders ain't just good for nutting people it is full of useless information including no doubt the date of the Battle of Hastings which to the unenlightened was ten sixty-six."

"Well this looks like this weekend will be the Second Battle of Hastings." Marshy declared

"That my son could well be true." Bandy Malc confirmed.

For Steve, the news was it was to be Hastings brought a smile to his face. He had spent many summer holidays with his grandparents a few miles outside of Hastings and just across the Kent border in Hawkhurst. How many hours had he spent on Hastings beach or over at Camber Sands. For once he knew the town they would be heading for unlike Margate last May's Bank Holiday.

"Jinx here looks happy at least." Declared Big Ron, using Steve's nickname that had stuck with him for years despite most people never quite knowing how he had gained it.

"Got laid in Hastings last year. Picked up this bird and ended up at some party having it away in a bathroom, actually in the bathtub as every other space was occupied by couples fucking. Couldn't hear the music from the record player for the swish of pubic hair, if you know what I mean?"

"Last of the fucking romantics." Laughed Big Ron, and added, "Maybe you will get lucky again."

Since breaking up with last steady girlfriend, and the disastrous one-night stand with Sandra Dee things had not been going that well in that department. He had met his last serious girlfriend Pauline at the Warner's Holiday Camp at Dovercourt, where he and Bandy Malc had shared a chalet, more a wooden hut but it had been good fun. Pauline had been a little goer and a good looker; the only problem came after the holiday when she went home to Balham. That part of London was a shit hole and not the place to wander about after dark with Teddy Boys still in circulation who thought nothing of cutting up a Mod. Mostly they had met up in Soho at the Heaven and Hell Club in Old Compton Street where the music was loud and the downstairs dark. Lack of finances for the rail fare and the fact she was only fifteen hastened the end not to mention her two brothers who hadn't taken kindly to an 'outsider' with their little sister.

Steve admitted to himself that his one-line chat up lines had not been that successful recently and concluded that 'Hello darlin' do you fancy a shag?' probably needed to be worked on a bit.

"So, we all meet up at about 8:30 on Saturday morning. I reckon it will take about two and a half hours. Up to the new Dartford tunnel, down to Maidstone, then across country to Hastings. That's the way I went before and it should be a clear run." Steve postulated.

"Sounds good to me." Bandy Malc

"And that goes for the rest of us." Said Big Ron, gaining nods from the others.

"Gotta be better weather than Clacton last Easter. Jesus that was fucking cold and wet, never thought I was ever gonna warm up." Big Ron reminded everyone. "Coldest fucking Easter for over eighty years and all we had was our fucking parkas to keep warm and then it pissed down on fucking Sunday just to add to our pleasures." Steve added.

"It was alright for you. You had that bird who worked in the chemist to keep you warm." Bandy Malc commented with a wry smile on his face.

"Big mistake taking her, complained the whole time, I'm cold or I'm hungry or I'm wet. Taught me a lesson though, travel light, leave the birds at home."

"Didn't she chuck you?" Bandy Malc asked.

"Went off with a wanker from Romford who had an Austin A40 Farina, decided four wheels were better than two."

"That whole fucking town was dead, no shops open, and the pubs were only open from 12 to 2 even that fucking café that was open refused to serve us. East London on Sea was fucking closed for business. Never been so fucking bored. Only time I warmed up was when we stormed the pier." Big Ron reminisced.

"Even that was a waste of time. The coppers stepped in and spoiled the fun. Shit getting up to a bit of mischief was the only way to save you from freezing to death." Steve added.

"Then the Mirror newspaper calling us 'The Wild Ones', what a load of bollocks. Slightly 'miffed off' but hardly 'wild'." Sniggered Marshy.

Wishin' and Hopin'- The Mersey Beats.

It was Friday and it was payday and the day before the August Bank Holiday, so Steve was just ticking off the hours until he could get away from the factory.

"We gotta get this order out today", shouted the foreman, "One thousand special picture frames for Boots the Chemist, so, pull your fucking fingers out."

Each frame was sprayed white then with wire wool rubbed down and sprayed again before finishing, not the most intellectually challenging work, but it did allow Steve to think about the weekend.

"You takin a bird with you to 'astings?" shouted Roger, another young Mod on the next workbench.

"Flying solo. Too much grief takin a bird away." Replied Steve remembering his weekend in Clacton all too clearly.

"Don't blame you." Replied Roger.

"Not that I've got a bird." Steve said to himself, but wasn't gonna admit that to Roger.

"OK lunch break." The foreman shouted over the blaring radio.

"Jesus, I need a ciggie. Feels like today will never end."

The car park of the factory was where the employees escaped from the ever-present dust of the work floor which hung heavy in the air even as the extractors did their best to clear the air.

Across the car park Steve watched Paul from the accounts department, a real Ace Face and well known in the Southend scene walking towards his new scooter, a brand-new Vespa GS, Gran Sport 160.

Steve walked over and took a closer look, "Nice wheels."

Paul turned and looked at Steve with a distaste, who he considered just a ticket, someone still wearing last week's fashion, slightly grown-out hair and not enough or too any mirrors on his old scooter.

"Bet that cost you a few bob?" Steve commented.

"Paid cash for it, no fucking never-never for me." Paul boasted.

"Good for you, I still owe a bundle on mine." Steve admitted, looking towards his recently acquired Sportique.

"The better the scooter the better class of bird you pick up." Paul quipped.

"Cunt" thought Steve realising he was at the end of a put down and walked away.

"Thinks he is the fucking dog's bollocks, so far up his own fucking arsehole he can see light." Steve cursed silently.

Roger grinned hearing the utterance, and handed Steve another cigarette, "What do you expect?

"I wouldn't piss on him if he was on fire." Cursed Steve.

"That's what happens to you when you shag the boss's daughter."

"I wouldn't touch her with yours." Steve laughed.

"You know what they used to say about her when asked to get her knickers off, her reply, I have to get them out of me handbag first."

With the break over Steve returned to his work place, still seething with injustice and counting the minutes until they came around with the little brown envelopes.

It was six thirty Friday night and Ready Steady Go was de rigor watching for any Mod, catching the latest dance moves and new sounds plus of course for the boys to letch at Cathy McGowan, queen of the Mods.

"Stevie there's someone at the front door." Called Steve's mum from the kitchen.

"Fuck." Thought Steve as he detached himself from the black and white image on the TV and went to the front door.

"Wendy?" Steve said as he opened the door.

"Our TV's gone on the blink, can I come and watch Ready Steady Go with you?"

"OK, come on in." Steve said as he ushered her through to the lounge.

Wendy lowered herself down on the settee next to Steve and was glued to the screen. The Kinks performed their latest record, 'You Really Got Me' and Manfred Mann, their rendition of Do Wah Diddy Diddy which got the nod of approval from Steve and Wendy as they watched the selected studio audience gyrating to the latest moves.

"Shame the Beatles have knocked off the Rolling Stones from number one in the charts." Uttered Steve as the charts were announced.

"I like the Beatles, especially Paul." Wendy responded.

"All the little girls love Paul McCartney, but he ain't really a Mod, is he?"

"But he is so cute."

Steve raised his eyebrows and rolled his eyes pretending compete incomprehension of Wendy's crush on this pop idol.

Steve caught a whiff of her perfume and remembered that smell from when he had snogged her a couple of weeks ago. Being Bandy Malc's sister made him feel awkward, but she was up for it, and it took some self-control to stop him going too far.

When the program finished Wendy made it obvious she was available, but this was neither the time or place with his mum and dad in the kitchen.

"You can take me to Hastings with you." Wendy ventured.

Steve looked at her and knew that she was game for anything, but shook his head, "Sorry darlin' but me and Malc are going alone. There could be trouble this weekend and I can't take that chance."

"I wouldn't be any trouble, and we could have some fun."

"Another time maybe."

Wendy pulled a grimace, but knew she was in a losing battle to get off with Steve.

I Get Around-The Beach Boys

"You're up early Stevie, wasn't expecting you up before lunchtime." Steve's mum said as she walked through to the kitchen. In fact, Steve had hardly slept at all with thought of the weekend in front of him and had got up early to make some toast.
Steve took one last look in the hall mirror, new Levi's, button-down blue Ben Sherman shirt, grey jumper and his Clarke's Desert Boots, "Pretty neat", he said to himself as he wound his Southend College of Technology and Arts scarf around his neck and pulled on his original US Army fish-tail parka with the 'Southend Mods' emblazoned across the back with the obligatory Union Jack flag and its fur edged hood.
"Thought I would go down and see grandad and grandma. Fancy a trip out away from Southend for a change of scenery."
"I am sure they will be pleased to see you, send mum and dad my love, and here is a couple of quid to spend on yourself."
"Thanks Mum."
"Now stay out of trouble, you know what happens on Bank Holidays these days with you young people getting into all kind of scrapes."
"Don't worry Mum, I don't think Hawkhurst is likely to see any trouble."
"Now be careful on your scooter."
"Yes, I will."

Bandy Malc was waiting outside his house a few doors down as Steve rode down the road. Like Steve he was dressed in his parka, but topped off with a pork-pie hat that had become all the rage.
"My sister is mightily pissed off that you are not taking her with you." Bandy Malc reported.
"Wendy is only just fifteen, and your dad would kill me if anything happened to her and not coming home tonight would surely cause him some serious grief."
"You know she fancies you like mad? And says that she could say that she is going to spend the night with a friend."
"She is a pretty little thing that's for sure, but going out with your mate's sister is a recipe for trouble, and in any case this ain't the sort of trip for someone of her age where more than likely there is going to be some aggro and Clacton taught me to ride single"
"Spoken like a real gent." Admitted Bandy Malc, "Come on let's get going if we are gonna meet up with the rest of them.

Steve and Bandy Malc were the first to arrive at Southend Victoria station the designated meeting point for setting off.
Steve took the opportunity to light up a cigarette while they waited and looked out across the Victoria Circus roundabout the scene of his last encounter with the law.
"How many laps of the roundabout did you manage before you were stopped?" demanded Bandy Malc with a malicious smile on his face.

"Thirty. Then PC Plod jumped out and waved his arms at me to halt. Probably saying that I was lost after coming out from evening classes at the Southend College of Art and Technology was not the cleverest answer so he cuffed me across the head and told me to sod off."

"Aren't our policeman wonderful."

"Bollocks."

One by one the others arrived, Big Ron and Marshy on their Lambretta scooters, Mike Smith astride Steve's old tatty two-tone, green and rust 125, with Razzle one of the birds he picked up in the Harold Dog last weekend, and the girl that Steve had really fancied.

Steve patted his pocket to ensure he still had his stash of Purple Hearts which cost him ten bob for twenty to keep him going and a packet of Durex in case he got lucky.

Bandy Malc was showing off his chromed side panels to the envy of the others, plus the six mirrors and the four spotlights he had added, "Cost me half-a-crown a square inch to have them chromed."

Steve looked at his 1962 red Vespa Sportique, looking good with whip aerial now attached with of course an Esso Tiger Tail hanging limply from the top, but lack of funds had curtailed adding more accessories.

"Are we ready to roll?" Steve called out as cigarettes were stubbed out and the group climbed aboard their machines.

"The weekend starts here. Let 'em roll." Cried out Big Ron as he gunned his Lambretta onto the road with the others soon on his tail.

It was mid-morning as Steve and the others pulled into the car park at the Royal Oak Hotel in Hawkhurst, their numbers bolstered by about thirty other Mods on their scooters from Maidstone and Medway making their way to the coast.

Guests arriving at the hotel eyed the recent arrivals with a mixture of loathing and trepidation, and expecting trouble to break out at any moment.

"This is where I am gonna split for a couple of hours. Me grandparents live just down the road here so I want to see them as the old boy has been a bit poorly recently." Steve explained.

"You want us to come along?" Bandy Malc asked.

"Nah, it would be better if I went alone. Probably the old boy would have a heart attck if we all turned up."

"We can wait for you if you like?" Big Ron added.

"I can meet up with you later. In the town centre of Hastings there is a clock tower at a place called the Memorial, and I can hook up with you all at about four o'clock."

"OK we will keep a look out for you."

Steve mounted his scooter, waved and set off down the High Street towards Flimwell, the memories flooding back at the times he had trod this road as a kid. Now with his trusty stead and the wind in his face he felt on top of the world. This was going to be a great weekend.

His Grandpa's house was an old weather-boarded house facing a small green on the edge of Hawkhurst the venue for many happy holidays in his childhood. In the old days, he would play with the kids who came down from the East End for the hop picking on the farm across the road. Across the green was a small pub called the Sawyers Arms where he had spent many hours sitting on the outside step eating packets of Smith's crisps while his dad and grandpa had gone for an evening pint. The old man's eyes lit up when he opened the side door to see his only grandson standing there, "Come see who is here Nellie." He called to his wife.

"Stevie what a lovely surprise, come in. Do you want a coffee?"

"Yeah, love a cuppa, me mouth feels like the bottom of budgie cage."

"What you doing down here, are you coming to stay with us?" Nellie asked.

"No, just a flying visit. Off to join me mates for a day out at the seaside."

"How's your mum and dad?"

"Just fine. Me mum still works in the dressing gown factory and the Old Man commutes up to the Smoke every day."

"And you?"

"Still working in the picture framing factory which is dead boring but I am going to evening school to do me 'A' levels to get a better job."

"Good for you." Responded his Grandad.

"It's so good to see you, we didn't think we would see much of you now you are all grown up."

"I spent the happiest days of my life down here, even when I nearly drowned in the farmer's pond across the road." Steve laughed at the memory.

"You know you can stay for the night if you want to, we still have the spare bedroom."

"No, I am meeting me mates later, but thanks all the same."

"Look here's ten bob to buy yourself a decent meal tonight, we don't want you to go hungry do we, as there is nothing much of you to start with."

It was only just over four hundred yards after leaving his grandparent's house that Steve first noticed the girl standing on the pavement by a high hedge, her head down and her long brown hair covering her face or maybe it was the amount of leg she was showing in her mini-dress, but whatever it was he put the brakes on and stopped, "Are you OK?"

The girl slowly looked up and seemed to focus her large green eyes on Steve as he sat on his scooter.

"Where are you going? Do you want a lift?"

The girl peered back towards the direction of Flimwell and it was clear she was uncomfortable about something.

"Has your boyfriend ditched you or something?"

"I just needed to escape and get some air." She said in a heavily accented voice.

"You ain't from round here are you darling?" Steve asked trying to make out where she was from.

"London." She said.

"That's the weirdest fucking London accent I have ever fucking heard."

"I was born in Moscow, but live in London where my father works."

"You're Russian?"

A slightest smile crossed her face as she nodded and answered, "Yes I'm Russian but I have lived in London for over six years."

24

"Do you live here?" She asked

"No, I live near Southend."

"The south end of what?

"Southend on sea in Essex, I have just been to see my grandparents who live just down the road then I'm off to Hastings to meet up with my mates."

"You are going to Hastings now?" the girl asked

"Is that where you were heading?" Steve asked.

The girl hesitated for a moment, looked back down the road and nodded her head, "Yes Hastings will do just fine."

"Do you want a lift?"

Again, the girl hesitated, looked at the scooter, then at Steve before answering, "I have never ridden on a scooter before."

"Just hop on the back put your arms around my waist and hang on. It's as easy as that, when I lean over you lean the same way, OK?"

The girl walked over to the Vespa, hitched up her already short skirt and straddled the rear pillion seat.

"I don't even know what your name is, they call me Steve, what's yours?

"Nika."

"Hi Nika, pleased to meet you." Steve said feeling foolish even as he said it, here was a girl who looked just like Cathy McGowan and she was on the back of his scooter.

"Nifty." He said to himself as he kicked the Vespa into life and set off his body slightly bent forward, knees practically touching the front panel and toes pointing out in the Mod mode for riding a scooter and retraced his route back up to the High Street with Nika's arms wrapped about him.

Needles and Pins-The Searchers

By the time Steve and Nika reached the Sedlescombe junction to join the A21 he had to wait to join the steady armada of scooters heading towards Hastings. Hundreds of Mods were heading South. Laughter and the sound of the engines being revved to within an inch of their lives was the order of the day.

"This is what it is all about." Shouted Steve, a big grin covering his face, "Life don't get much better than this."

"Are these all your friends?" shouted Nika in Steve's ear.

"Not actually my friends but Mods, mostly from London by the look of their fancy suits under their parkas."

Riding under the Harrow Bridge gave Steve and Nika the first view of the sea as the rode down Sedlescombe Road North, which somehow looked bluer than the Thames Estuary off Southend.

Nika had relaxed a bit from when they had first started off in Hawkhurst and seemed to be enjoying the experience.

Steve looked at his watch and hoped the gang had waited for him as picking up his passenger had slowed him down a bit.

"Do you think your friends will be alright with me being with you?" Nika questioned, a slight nervousness in her voice.

"I think they will be fucking jealous." Steve thought to himself, but answered that he thought they would be just fine.

"Do you mind if I stay with you as I do not know anybody here?"

"Weren't you going to meet somebody here in Hastings?" Steve questioned.

"No, I just wanted to escape from my parents for a while, they keep such close control of my life and I wanted to see what life was really all about."

"That's twice you have used the word 'escape', are your parents that protective of you?"

"I am driven to school, taken to the shops so I never get to see what life is really like by myself."

"Well welcome to my life." Steve jested.

Finding somewhere to park the scooter proved to be a challenge but finally Steve found a place near the cricket ground.

"I said that I would meet my friends down by the Memorial, but I never thought there would be so many Mods here. Everywhere you look is a sea of khaki parkas, in fact more than had been present at Clacton or Margate.

"What do they look like?" Nika asked.

"That's the problem, everyone here looks much the same, the way they dress makes it difficult to find them."

"Hey Jinx, over here." Came Bandy Malc's instantly recognisable voice,

"Why did he call you Jinx?"

"A nickname from way back when everything I did seemed to be a disaster."

"Where the fuck have you been? we've been waiting for ages." Bemoaned Big Ron.

"Got a bit side-tracked, I want you to meet Nika."

"Leave him alone for a few hours and he turns up with the most gorgeous bird. How the fuck did he do that?" Marshy demanded.

Mike Smith's girlfriend Pam Haswell or Razzle as she was better known, took a long look at the girl Steve had picked up and walked around her, studying her clothes. "Shit this girl has class, what the fuck does she see in you?"

"Sparkling personality, titillating conversation, her knight in shining armour." Steve boasted.

"Look at her shoes, this girl has all the latest fab gear." Declared Razzle.

"And she is Russian." Added Steve.

"Well she don't look Russian." Commented Big Ron.

"How would you know what a fucking Russian looks like?" Razzle fired back at him.

"I've seen the James Bond film and that Rosa Klebb bird and them Russian women athletes who look like they are built like brick shithouses."

"That hardly makes you an expert on Russian birds does it?" Razzle concluded.

"What language does she speak?" Marshy asked.

Nika turned towards him a big smile on her face, "Whatever language you like. French, German, English and Russian and I can get by in Spanish, so make your choice."

"We'll settle for English. Now let's get some grub I'm fucking starving, my stomach thinks my throat has been cut." Marshy replied.

"Fish and chips from along the seafront by the fishing huts." Steve suggested, as he grabbed Nika's hand which to his surprise she did not pull away and started to move off in the direction of the Old Town.

Nika turned to Steve and whispered, I like your friends they seem so genuine and honest."

"I dunno about that but we've known each other for a long time now and you can rely on them in any situation."

"You are lucky to have such good friends. Tell me about the Rockers." Nika asked.

"Well they ride motorbikes, dress from head to toe in leather and seem to resent us Mods for our clothes and music.

"I saw in the newspapers and television that you fight the Rockers."

"What kind of sheltered life do you lead?"

"My father is very strict and protective that's why I'm enjoying myself so much here with you and your friends."

"Don't believe everything you read in the papers, the press just blew everything out of proportion and encouraging kids to fight for their cameras, some even got paid to get a good picture of some Mod getting a real kicking."

"So, will there be trouble here?" Nika wondered.

"There are always some who want a bundle, but I ain't seen that many Rockers about."

"So, we now go to restaurant to eat?"

"Not exactly. We are going to buy fish and chips and eat them out of newspaper on the beach.

"Like a picnic?"

"Yeah like a picnic." Steve concluded.

Walking across the road clasping their bags of fish and chips the friends tried to find some shade as the afternoon sun was now quite warm, the sudden sound stopped them dead in their tracks. A noise like rumbling thunder coming down the Old London Road, then they came into view, a hundred or more motorbikes riding four or five abreast.

As they passed the assembled Mods the abuse started, shouting and swearing emanating from both groups, but no attempt to stop them.

"Are they the Rockers?"

Steve looked and Nika, her heavily black eyeliner giving her bright green eyes a beautiful frame as she watched the leather clad riders go past.

"Hey Steve, didn't know we had requested the cavalry."

Steve turned to see his old friend Col a Mod from Hastings he had met last year on holiday, "Thought you country folk might need some assistance."

"Praise be the Lord we are saved from the ravishing horde." Col added sarcasm heavy in his voice, "Where you staying?"

"We only got here an hour or so ago, so we ain't made any arrangements yet."

"My parents are away, you can crash at my place if you want?"

"Are you sure? Wot about me mates?"

"They will have to make do with the floor, but yeah, OK."

"We could stay in a hotel." Nika suggested.

"If it is anything like Margate or Clacton they shut their fucking doors when they see a Mod."

"I have money to pay." Nika said producing a wad of notes from her small handbag."

Steve quickly covered her hand holding the bank notes before anyone could see the thick roll of notes. "It's OK we can stay at Col's pad along the seafront near that big white building. We don't need money for that."

 "Anyone want to doss down at Col's place tonight?" Steve asked.

Razzle poked Mike in the ribs, "Yeah we will, I don't fancy sleeping under the pier on those fucking hard stones." She said, "And I am sure Nika here feels the same. So, thanks for the offer."

Nika nodded her head in agreement.

"I think me, Big Ron and Marshy here might go on the hunt for some talent." Bandy Malc concluded, "You never know some of Jinx's good luck might have rubbed off on us."

Why Not Tonight-Mojos

"You know the Rolling Stones are on the pier tonight? Do you wanna go?" Col asked.
"Can you get tickets?
"Yeah, ten bob each." Col replied.
"Do wanna see the Stones? Steve turned towards Mike and Razzle who were both nodding as was Nika.
"Can you get four?"
"Can't see that will be a problem. I know the guys on the pier, they will get us in." Col answered confidently.

During the late afternoon more and more Mods arrived streaming down Queen's Road on their scooters towards the sea front, the sun glinting on the chrome adding to the impression of knights of old preparing for battle.
"We should join in the fun, it'll be great to join all the scooters driving around town." Said Steve as he looked at Nika.
"Where are they going?" Nika asked.
"Nowhere in particular, just showing off their scooters and to be part of the whole thing and showboating."
"Showboating?" Nika asked looking confused.
"Showing off." Steve explained.
"I don't understand." Nika added."
"Like a parade, just a bit of fun. Now let's go and get my scooter."
By the time they got back to the cricket ground where Steve had left the scooter and the sight of two Rockers standing by his Vespa did not bode well.
Pushing Nika behind him he approached the Rockers his hands clenched into fists as he went to retrieve his scooter, "You touch my scooter at your own risk." he shouted.
"You didn't say that when I put the fucking clutch back together for you."
"Fred what the fuck are you doing here?" demanded Steve.
"Just making sure nobody decided to trash your wheels."
"But these are Rockers." Nika declared.
"Fred is a friend, probably my best friend, that is after you make an exception for his clothes sense and the fact he rides a motorbike."
"But you are supposed to be enemies."
"This is Nika, "Steve hesitated before continuing as he worked out how to introduce her further, "A girl I met on the road."
"Some people get all the luck." Said the second Rocker, eyeing Nika up and down.
"This is Paul who hails from Brighton, the owner of a beautiful BSA Royal Star." Said Fred. "Like you I met him and his girlfriend Chrissy on the road, but I think you got the better deal." He said looking directly at Nika.
"Why do you fight if you are friends?" Nika asked.
"We don't actually fight each other if that's what you mean? Explained Steve.
"The press needed something to put on their front pages, and Mods and Rockers gave them something to write about." Fred explained.

"The word is out that things are likely to kick off tomorrow, so keep out of trouble and don't go down near the Bathing Pool." Paul advised.

Hiking up her skirt to get onto the scooter, Fred gave Steve a discreet wink and added "Don't do anything I wouldn't do."

Steve kick started the Vespa, gave Fred the finger and let out the clutch and accelerated away.

"Lucky bastard." Fred thought as he watched the Vespa drive out of sight.

There must have been hundreds of scooters cruising along the seafront down to the Old Town, past the fishing net huts to the car park near the West Hill Lift, a funicular railway that climbed to Hastings Castle high above them, then retracing their route back along the seafront.

Steve was exhilarated to be part of a show of strength of the Mods, part of a movement of youth sticking their fingers up to the establishment, and the police seemed helpless to do anything about it.

"This could never happen in Russia." Nika shouted into Steve's ear.

"This ain't Russia."

Just One Look- The Hollies

"I can take you home to your parents if you want me to?" Offered Steve.

Nika looked at him long and hard before answering, "This is first time in my life that I have been free to do what I want. It is so different to what I am used to and to be honest I am enjoying my freedom."

"But what will your parents think?"

"I think that they will be worried, especially my father."

"We could find a phone box and ring them to say that you are safe."

"I don't think that would be a good idea."

"But you know what parents are like, just to hear you might make them feel better. I know my mum worries about me and often stays awake until I get home in the early hours of the morning before she goes to sleep."

"My parents hardly know that I am there at all, they send me to boarding school for young ladies to keep me out of the way. My father works all day and most of the night and my mother spends her time shopping and drinking Vodka."

"But they must love you."

Nika shrugged her shoulders.

It only took a few minutes to drive along the seafront to get to Col's parent's house in Undercliff Terrace in the shadow of the huge white Marina building, and already there were a couple of scooters parked out front including one he recognised, Mike's tatty 125.

Col said that the front door key would be under an upturned flowerpot if he had not returned, but the door was already ajar, and the pair entered.

The girl stood inside of the front door looked far from welcoming, "Who invited you?" she said her tone far from friendly.

"Colin invited us, my name is Steve and this is Nika."

"It's alright Linda, they are friends." Came Col's voice from the front room.

"Is she the Russian bird you talked about?" asked Linda turning to Col who had come out into the hallway.

"Excuse Linda she is half Polish and has no great love for the Russians."

"Przepraszam, że nie chcę cię obrazić" Said Nika.

"You speak Polish?" Linda said in surprise.

"Just a little." Admitted Nika.

"Wejdź."

Steve looked in amazement at Nika's linguistic skills, "I thought you said that you only spoke. French, German, English and Russian and a little Spanish?"

"And also, a little Polish." She giggled.

"Grab a beer and make yourself comfortable." Col offered as he sank back onto the settee and joined by Linda, "Looks like everything is gonna heat up tomorrow. Loads of Rockers are still pouring into the town,"

Razzle looked across at Nika who had hardly spoken since she arrived, "Are you alright luv?"

"I'm not used to this beer, it tastes strange."

"She is Russian so she probably wants a Vodka." Quipped Linda.

"I think the old man has a bottle in his drinks cabinet, I remember seeing it at Christmas. Ah here it is, Cossack Vodka." Col said as he half-filled a tumbler and handed it to Nika, who sniffed it before downing it in one gulp.

"Think the girl has a bit of a thirst on her. Give her another." Razzle demanded.

"Come get ready we gotta get down the pier to see the show." Said Col.

"You got tickets OK?"

"No problem. It's not what you know more who you know." Col said tapping the side of his nose.

Leaving their scooters, the three couples walked along the promenade towards the pier and it was soon obvious by the long queue that stretched from the 'The Happy Ballroom' all the way down to Bottle Alley that tonight was a sell-out.

"Don't worry about the queue, I got this worked out." Boasted Col, as they walked past the long line of fans, boosted in number because of the holiday weekend with out of towners who had taken advantage of the opportunity to see their heroes.

Near the front of the line Col halted his friends as he looked for someone.

"Here Col." Came the call from a tall Mod with his girlfriend, "Come and join us."

Even as they pushed into the line it was obvious that their intrusion was seriously pissing off those behind, including Paul the Ace Face from Steve's work and his girlfriend Pamela the boss's daughter.

"You fucking can't just push in, we've been queuing for ages. Get the fuck out of it."

Mick the tall Mod turned and walked back towards Paul, the look on his face and his balled fists should have warned him that his intentions were far from friendly.

"You got a problem arsehole?"

"This is a fucking queue, you just can't let these people push in."

"These are my friends, and I was saving a place for them. Understand?"

"Even him?" Paul pointed towards Steve."

Mick turned and looked back at Steve and Nika, winked and turned back face to face with Paul."

"As I said, I was saving a place for my friends, is there something in that statement you have difficulty in understanding?"

Realising that any further discussion was going to end up in violence Paul took the line of least resistance and shut up, but not before giving Steve a look that he would certainly not forget this incident.

Turning to others in the queue Mick simply asked, "Anyone else got a problem with me mates joining me?"

The shuffling of feet and downward eyes seemed to indicate that nobody else was willing to take up the challenge.

It was only a short wait before the line began moving and the friends were soon inside the ballroom waiting in anticipation for the arrival of the Rolling Stones.

"The third time the Stones have been to Hastings." Added Col

"Saw the Stones with the Everly Brothers and Bo Diddley last October at the Odeon in Southend." Steve added, "Bloody fantastic.".

"Did you watch Ready Steady Go on Thursday, The Kinks singing You Really Got Me, Manfred Mann belting out Do Wha Diddy Diddy.?" Asked Col.

"Everybody watches Ready Steady Go." Laughed Steve.

Nika laughed, she felt relaxed and safe among her new friends, something she had never experienced before or the freedom that came with it.

"Why do you like the Rolling Stones?" Steve asked

"They are unconventional and their music gritty and down to earth, added to that my father hates them. Anyway, there is nothing like Rhythm and Blues in Russia"

"Most parents hate them." added Col, "Too anti-establishment and not clean cut like The Beatles, just long-haired layabouts as my dad calls them."

"I brought 'Come On' when I first heard it on Radio Luxemburg, just about summed up my life at the time." Steve admitted.

Razzle looked at Nika and then at Steve and added, "Well it looks like your luck has changed now."

Without thinking about it Steve leant forward and kissed Nika on the lips, her mouth yielding, her tongue active against his, her arms wrapped about him her breasts pressed hard against him.

Steve pulled away and looked into her green eyes that seemed to dance in the light and he put his arms around her.

"Some people get all the fucking luck." Quipped Mike as Razzle gave him one of her looks.

For the first time Steve looked at Nika, not just as a casual bird he had picked up. Yes, she was stunningly pretty girl but there was something else about her, a warmth and a mystery, something he found hard to put into words.

Not Fade Away- The Rolling Stones

It was after eleven as Steve and Nika walked slowly hand in hand along the prom back to Col's place. It was still warm and they were in no hurry. In fact, Steve was still buzzing from the live performance and that was without the aid of Purple Hearts.
The supporting groups, The Worrying Kind and The Sabres both of which seemed to be well known to the patrons of the Happy Ballroom had only added to the evening. But it was the Stones rendition of the former Number One, 'It's all over now' that nearly brought the house down.
"What is going to happen tomorrow?" Nika asked.
"Nothing much. Most the Mods will meet up near or under the pier, just chatting having a joke and then probably doing much the same as today, cruising the streets of Hastings and St Leonards on Sea."
"And the Rockers?"
"If they know what is good for them they will probably stay at home but I expect they will make an appearance sometime." Steve said, trying to play down any thoughts of violence, although he knew very that there was a small minority of Mods that were there just to get into a fight.
"What about your friend Fred, he is a Rocker?" Nika wondered.
"He can look after himself, he ain't stupid."
"I hope he does not get hurt because he is your friend and I remember seeing in the newspapers about the fighting.".
"Don't believe everything you read in the newspapers, they hyped everything up to look worse than it really was, faking violent fighting scenes to sell their papers."
"It is the same in Russia, they only tell us what they want us to know, the press in the west has more freedom."
"The press here just want to make money and if that means bending the truth a bit they will do it."
It was the early hours before everybody decided to turn in, Col directed Razzle and Mike, then Steve and Nika into separate bedrooms upstairs, the bog is the last door on the right."
"You sleep on the bed and I will kip down on the floor." Said Steve.
"Why you want to sleep on the floor?" Nika asked.
"I hardly know you." Steve answered.
"So, you do not fancy me?"
Steve nearly chocked as he desperately tried to think of an appropriate response, "Of course I fancy you, you are the most beautiful girl I have ever met."
Nika looked Steve straight in the eye and said, "So now we have sex?"
Steve stood for a moment speechless, pinched himself to see if he was actually still awake and turned towards Nika who was already undressing.
"Are Russian girls always this straightforward?"
Nika smiled and answered, "I thought the English expression was if you don't ask you don't get."
Nika stood just in her bra and panties looking absolutely stunning and it was already having an effect on Steve, in spite of the beer he had consumed. This was not going to be a grope in the back row of the Regal Cinema in Rayleigh or a repeat of the bathroom episode.

"Wait I have something." as he reached into his jean's pocket for the packet of three Durex he had brought at the barber's the previous weekend.

Nika laughed as she saw the packet in Steve's hand as he tried with shaking hands to free a condom from its wrapper.

"You don't need those things." She giggled, "I told my mother that my periods were irregular and so she took me to our doctor who put me on a pill, that also happens to be the contraceptive pill."

"So, I don't need these?" Steve asked the embarrassment in his voice clearly evident.

"No. Now come over here and get into bed."

Steve thought to himself that it would be rude not to comply with Nika's request and slid between the sheets, feeling the warmth of her body close to him.

You Really Got Me-The Kinks.

From Undercliff Terrace you could hear the motorbikes roaring along the seafront and the sound brought Steve back to his senses.

"Shit its started." He said more to himself than the naked body of Nika lying next to him.

The memory of the night before brought a wicked smile to his face as he lit up a cigarette and peered out of the bedroom window across the promenade.

"The Rockers are on the move and we should go and find the others." He declared.

Leaving Nika to get ready, Steve went downstairs to make a coffee, and Razzle took the opportunity to pop in and see her. Immediately she noticed Nika's 'Peachy' dress hanging over the back of a chair and picking it up she had a good look at it, looking inside at the label, "It's a real Mary Quant, dress, shit that must have cost a fortune."

"Try it on, we are about the same size." Said Nika handing Razzle the minidress.

Razzle slipped the dress over her shoulders and looked at herself in the full-length bedroom mirror, a big smile across her face. "What I'd give for to own a dress like this." She proclaimed.

"Then do me a swop, give me your jeans and top and we will call it a deal."

"But my stuff is just brought in the high street, it ain't designer labelled like this, are you sure?"

"It looks better on you than it did on me." Nika said as she watched Razzle turn around in front of the dressing table mirror.

By the time the girls had slapped on some makeup they were ready to go.

"The promenade is still crawling with Rockers so I think we better take another route into town, follow me and Linda up around White Rock Gardens and down to the Memorial and hope to find the rest of your mates." Colin suggested.

The town was filling with Mods and Rockers, scooters and bikes everywhere, weaving in and out of the traffic and there seemed to be more police about than last night trying to keep the two factions apart.

Steve kept his eyes skinned for his mates but it was difficult with so many Mods about, "Like looking for a needle in a haystack." he said to himself.

"There. Over there I saw Bandy Malc, looks like he was having some aggro with a group of Rockers." Shouted Mike, who easily spotted his friend with his gait that earned him his nickname.

Pulling over and parking their scooters the three couples rushed over to the edge of the beach where Mike had spotted them.

"I'll give you five bob each to give me a couple of realistic photos, you know a bit of action."

Bandy Malc turned as he heard Steve arrive and smiled, "You look like the cat that got the fucking cream, but more of that later, this gentleman of the Evening Standard is trying to encourage us to start a fight and has offered us money to make it look real."

Even as Bandy Malc was talking a large Rocker walked up to the persistent reporter, wrenched the camera out of his hands and lobbed it into the sea, "That's what I think of your fucking deal, now piss off before you find out what a kicking is all about, and if you want real fighting pictures why don't you fuck off to Vietnam you spineless shit."

Looking at the Rocker then in the direction his camera had taken he decided to take the 'fuck off' option, and retreated to find more cooperative Mods and Rockers.

The Rocker took a small bow as the Mods clapped their hands.

"Right now, back to business. What do you lot want?" demanded the large Rocker.

"Does it hurt when you drag your knuckles on the ground when you walk?" asked Bandy Malc, the sarcasm heavy in his voice.

The Rocker laughed, "They hurt more when I've whacked a Mod."

"Yeah, but you gotta catch 'em first."

"So, you volunteering to find out?"

"The bigger they come the harder they fall."

The Rocker stepped forward, the intent obvious on his face, and it was not to shake his hand.

Steve stood back, he had seen Bandy Malc fight before and he knew what was coming. Springing forward Bandy Malc used his head and butted the Rocker on his head with full force on his nose. Normally that was enough to deter further aggression but in this instance the Rocker stood there wiped the blood from his nose and smiled, "So what else you gonna try?"

Shocked at the capacity to survive the head butt, Bandy Malc looked at the others and deciding discretion was the better part of valour, the Southend Mods took to their heels with the Rocker in hot pursuit, soon joined by a few of his mates who had been standing back watching.

Within a hundred yards the odds changed when the handful of Rockers came face to face with about thirty Mods who then became the chasers.

All along the shingle beach small groups of Mods and Rockers attempted to give each other a beating, fists flying and some putting the boot in.

Within minutes, hundreds had joined the rampage, charging across the stone beach, scattering deck chairs and holiday makers in all directions.

The ebb and flow of the fighting only changing when one side or the other had the majority in numbers.

From the corner of his eye Steve noticed Paul the Ace Face from work being dunked into the sea by a group of rockers and for a moment thought to go and assist, then thought better of it. He certainly didn't look like a high number now as he knelt in the surf, his hand-made suit looking the worse for its immersion in the sea. Steve wished he had a camera just to show him the photo the next time the arsehole did the superior Mod thing.

A few unlucky Mods and Rockers had gained a few bruises and cuts, some had gained a punching but on the whole few casualties were taken by either side and the sudden appearance of a load of police on the beach soon curtailed the fun.

"The coppers are fucking everywhere." Bemoaned Big Ron who collapsed on the beach fighting for breath after his activities. "I tell you what, I don't think I'm coming back here."

"I am sure the good citizens of Hastings would only be too pleased to hear that." Joked Steve.

Large crowds of youngsters now stood around while police tried to keep the warring factions apart, while all the time more and more vans disgorged even more coppers into the area.

Steve turned to Nika who had become very quiet, "Are you alright?"

"I don't think these shoes from Ravel were made for beach ware, my feet are killing me and I am going for a paddle in the sea,", with that she kicked off her shoes and headed slowly down the stony beach.

"Hang on Nika I will come with you." Steve shouted after her.

"Why are your beaches so stony?" Where is the sand?" Nika asked.

"There is a sandy beach a few miles from here where I used to come with my mum when I was young, but most holiday makers are just happy to be at the seaside eating ice creams and trying to get a suntan."

"Is there a beach at Southend on Sea?" Nika inquired.

"Well sort of, but then the sea goes on for one and half miles leaving mud."

"That does not sound very inviting."

"Well it ain't the south of France if that's what you mean."

What will you do after the weekend?"

"Go home and back to work, I suppose."

"I think I will probably be in trouble when I go back, but I have seen what life is really like and have enjoyed it."

"Can we meet again after this weekend, when you go back to London."

Nika looked Steve in the eye and shook her head, "I think that could be difficult."

"I don't mind coming up to London to see you. We could go to a few clubs and have some fun." Steve persisted.

Most of the rest of the afternoon saw the two rival factions riding through the town, while police did their best to keep them apart while some already bored were returning home or moving on to Brighton to see what was happening there.

Running the gauntlet past the Yelton Hotel on the seafront where the Rockers massed hurling abuse at the mounted Mods and anything else that came to hand Steve continued westwards towards St Leonards on Sea.

Getting bored the small group of Southend Mods pulled into Warrior Square just off the seafront to decide what to do next, and was soon joined by Col and his mates.

"Looks like the fun is over and I am getting bored just riding about. "Mike declared.

"We could go into town to a coffee bar I know that has some good music on their jukebox and the coffee ain't bad." Col suggested.

"Fuck all else to do with fucking coppers everywhere, even saw some white helmeted coppers from Brighton and the rumour is that they are flying even more in from London to deal with the disturbance." Moaned Bandy Malc.

"They seem to be stopping everybody and suggesting they go home, but something else is going on. They appear to be looking and asking questions about a missing girl in particular. Got a photo they are showing around."

Back in town the group headed down to the Memorial then to a doorway next to a Burton's tailors.

"Quick go up these stairs, there's a coffee bar up there." Shouted Col as he entered the doorway and led the group up the steep narrow stairwell.

Steve remembered the club from his visit the previous year, The Pam Dor was an OK place, dark dingy with a good selection on the jukebox.

"Bit like the Harold Dog but above ground." Bandy Malc commented as he pushed his way through the crowd.

Nika pushed a pound note into Steve's hand as he neared the counter, "Buy drinks for everyone." She whispered.

"Eight coffee's luv." Demanded Steve, "And some change for the juke box."

"Load the jukebox with some good music Col." Said Steve as he handed him a handful of sixpenny pieces."

To the sound of the Animal's singing the House of the Rising Sun the friends sipped their coffee from their Pyrex cups and decided what to do next.

"Are we gonna stick it out here or bugger off someplace else" Marshy asked as he looked round the table for a response.

"What about riding up to Margate? or along to Brighton?" Big Ron suggested.

"I think I will stick here with Nika." Steve answered.

"Don't blame you mate, if I had found a bird like her I would stay as well." Bandy Malc said.

Mike after a poke in the ribs from Razzle added that they would stay in Hastings as well.

The appearance of three girls who had just arrived through the smoke-filled gloom suddenly made the idea of leaving redundant as Bandy Malc switched into chat-up mode, "Hello darlings. Wanna a coffee?"

"It's alright Shirl, he is from Essex but is house trained I am reliably informed." Called Col to one of the girls.

"There's a party tonight up at house on the park, Upper Park Road, you know it?" shouted Shirl above the music.

"Sounds cool. You all going?"

"Yeah should be a good bash."

"Fancy going to a party?" Steve said as he turned to Nika.

"Da, sorry I mean yes." She replied at the opportunity of another new experience.

Bandy Malc, Marshy and Big Ron had now turned on their charm at the thought of meeting some new girls and the possibility of a leg-over later.

The girls in turn looked somewhat bemused at the attention they were receiving from these out of town Mods.

"My mum warned me about Northerners." Declared Shirl.

"Southend ain't up North." Stated Bandy Malc.

"It's north of the fucking Thames." One of the other girls added.

Bandy Malc just slapped his head with his hand, knowing he was on the losing side of the argument and one that he was not going to win.

Col laughed and added, "You never heard the expression, Sussex born and Sussex bred, strong in arm and thick in head."

"Whose side are you on Col?" demanded Shirl and added," Remember you live here when this lot go home, so watch it."

Col turned to Steve and beckoned him closer, "You wanna earn a few bob this evening before we go partying?"

"Doing what?" demanded Steve.

"Same as we did last summer down the Bingo Hall in the Old Town."

"Is your mate still running that scam?"

"Yeah, but he is clever enough just to use it on the low paid out prizes."

"What if he got caught?"

"He reckons he could drop the tray of balls quick enough so nobody could prove anything."

"So, we go along and buy half a dozen Bingo cards, select one and at half time pass my mate on the stairs who takes a quick look, commits the numbers to memory, then you just wait for him to read out the numbers and claim your winnings, shout 'House' and collect your thirty quid."

"Sounds good to mc." Declared Steve, and added, "We will take the girls back to your place and they can do whatever it is they do to get ready for the party."

It was a rerun of what Col and Steve did last summer, and after the game was over they would split the winnings fifty-fifty with Col's mate, the Bingo caller and end up with about fifteen quid better off.

I'm into something good- Herman's Hermits

It was not hard to find the party in Upper Park Road, the parked scooters and the music blaring out of the house made it fairly obvious.

"Looks like we are just in time to liven it up a bit." Said Bandy Malc now with Shirl hanging on his arm.

The big guy at the door did not seem the welcoming type as Bandy Malc tried to push through.

"No fucking gate crashers." He growled.

"It's alright we are friends of Sarah, we're invited." Explained Shirl, "Come on Bill. You know me, Colin and Linda here plus a couple of his mates, we don't mean no trouble."

"Well no trashing the joint."

The house was crammed full, the Dansette record player was cranked up to full volume in the front room where couples were shuffling to Louie Louie by the Kingsmen.

"You wanna dance?" Steve said as he pulled Nika into the crowded front room, "I love this song."

Hardly room to swing a cat, Nika kicked off her shoes and threw her arms round Steve's neck and pushed her body close to his and gyrated to the music.

"Here take a few of these, they will keep you going." Steve said as he handed her four Purple Hearts. Hang on I'll get you some water."

The kitchen had the heavy smell of pot where everyone appeared to be toking on a joint as he found a glass and filled it with water, threw a hand full of Hearts in his own mouth and a swig of water before topping the glass up again.

"Don't suppose you got any to spare?" came a voice from behind him.

Steve turned to find Sarah standing in front of him, the girl he had met the year before in Hastings.

"How many do you want?"

"Any you can spare."

Steve tipped half a dozen into her open hand.

"Don't suppose you wanna see the bathroom?" she joked, but with a mischievous glint in her eye.

"I don't think the bird I am with would appreciate that."

"Shame. Thanks for the uppers."

Nika was still dancing by herself when Steve returned although the music had changed.

"Here take some water with the pills."

She looked at the small purple heart-shaped tablets in the palm of her hand, "What are these?"

"Uppers that fight off tiredness and give you a buzz."" Explained Steve.

Nika nodded and put them in her mouth and washed them down with the water.

"Now let's go and find something a bit stronger to drink."

Dawn was breaking when they arrived back on Col's parent's house. The culmination of the Purple Hearts and alcohol were beginning to wear off and getting their heads down for a couple of hours seemed to be the priority of the moment.

Razzle and Mike had decided to stay with the others at the party as they were both too pissed and spaced out to ride Mike's scooter back to Col's pad and were sleeping it off there.

Nika stood by the window and watched the sun rise and knew the weekend was drawing to a close.

"I'm cold." She said hugging herself.

"I thought you Russian girls were used to the cold."

"Yes, it gets cold in Chelsea." She laughed.

"But this is August during an English summer, and it don't get much better than this. Come here I will make you warm." Steve offered.

Nika climbed under the bedclothes and snuggled up to Steve, feeling the warmth of his body against her and was soon asleep.

Steve lay his head on his hand propped up on his elbow as he ran his finger over Nika's breasts and down across her flat tummy until he reached her pubic hair. Their lovemaking had not been like his earlier forays with the opposite sex, this time it just seemed more natural, both seeking gratification from each other.

Nika opened her eye wide, her green eyes questioning, "So you want us to have sex again?"

Steve laughed as he thought it must be Christmas come early, "No I just wanted to look and touch you. I have never met a girl like you before."

"But you must have had plenty of girls?"

"Not like you, they were different, a fumble in the back row of the cinema or at some party when everybody was drunk or high, not really romantic, a bit of a macho thing, pulling birds was a challenge, then bragging about it."

"What makes me different?"

"Everything, you are Russian, sophisticated, clever and not one of usual Mod birds I mix with."

"But you have fun in your life?"

"Life is more like a challenge, making your money last the week, trying to keep up with the latest trends and not be thought of as a ticket."

"A ticket?"

"Yeah, a ticket is a mod who ain't totally up to date with everything with last week's styles, not into the latest sounds."

"But does that matter to your friends?"

"None of us are high numbers, but we try."

"High numbers?"

"The trendiest Mods, not your everyday type."

"Does it matter?"

"It does to some of them."

"Is that why Razzle got excited about my dress?"

"Are you kidding, the latest Mary Quant dress is what every Mod girl dreams of, but working behind the counter in Woolworth's, Razzle would have to save for months to even think about buying one."

"Then I think I will let her keep it, I like her, she is not like the other girls I know. She is kind and not bitchy."

"So, what about your friends?" Steve asked.

"The other girls at college are from rich families, spoilt, get what they want,"

"Is your father rich?"

Nika hesitated, "Compared to most Russians he is well off, but he works all the time and compensates by letting me buy whatever I want. "He paid for me and my mother to go and see the Beatles film a Hard Day's Night."

"Yeah I saw it the other week in Southend."

"No, he paid for us to go to première at the London Pavilion, fifteen guineas a seat."

"Shit, I saw that on the TV, the première was attended by The Beatles and their wives and girlfriends, and a host of important guests including Princess Margaret and Lord Snowdon, your old man must have some pretty good connections to get tickets for that."

"I would rather have seen it with you and your friends." Nika said softly, "Too many stuffy people who were only there to be seen, not to watch the film

"Saw the Beatles last year live at the Odeon in Southend, had to queue all night for the fucking tickets."

"Are they your favourite group? Nika asked.

"They're OK, not really a Mod band though

"My friends in Russia are so jealous of me here in London, and I send them the latest Beatle albums which are impossible to buy in Moscow and when I can I send Levi jeans, real ones not the fakes they sell at home."

"Do you miss your friends?" Steve inquired.

"Of course, I do, I'm a foreigner here. You are so lucky to have your friends around you."

"You know you will always have some new friends here."

The frantic raping on the front door soon brought everybody awake and Steve could hear Mike down in the hallway. Something was wrong.

"What's happened?" Steve shouted as he came down the stairs.

"Look at this." Mike said holding up the newspaper.

Steve scanned the Daily Mirror headlines, 'Riot Police Fly To Seaside'

"That explains all the coppers."

"No, not that read further down and look at the photo."

Staring out from the page was a photo of a younger Nika and below the caption, 'Russian Diplomat's daughter abducted in Kent. Nika Petrova went missing on Saturday around midday and police are conducting searches to find her. Reports that she was seen riding on the back of a scooter in the direction of Hastings have not been confirmed, but investigations continue'.

"Jesus Fucking Christ. What the fuck is going on here?" cried Steve.

From the top of the stairs dressed only in a pair of knickers and Steve's Ben Sherman shirt, Nika stood, tears in her eyes.

"Is this true? Are you this diplomat's daughter?"

Nika lowered her eyes and nodded.

"What the fuck was a Russian Diplomat's daughter doing wandering around in Hawkhurst?" Steve demanded.

"There is a secret Russian Embassy residence at Flimwell, Seacox House, where diplomats and Embassy staff can take time out from London. The KGB look after security and the American CIA keep an eye on who comes and goes." Nika explained.
"This sounds like a fucking James Bond film with KGB and CIA involved."
"I was so bored and when I said that I escaped I was telling the truth. I went out for a walk in the grounds and got out through a gap in the perimeter fence, without being seen, and when I passed a couple of Americans up near the main road, they just wolf-whistled and made some obscene suggestions. So, I just kept walking and that is when I met you."
"Didn't you realize what trouble you could get into, and for that matter the deep shit that I am now in?"
"It would be hard for you to understand what my life was like. I had no freedom. If I went shopping I had a KGB minder. At Cheltenham College for Young Ladies, I was kept separate from the other girls except for lessons and watched all the time. I had no life. You have freedom to do want you want. I envy girls like Razzle she has a life."
"And now what do we do?" Steve demanded.
"I think I will have to go back." Nika said her head bowed, a tear in her eye.

By midday the whole group had assembled at Col's parent's house at Undercliff Terrace and now knowing the whole story tried to work out a solution.
Nika sat with Razzle's arm around her, trying to comfort her.
"The police are herding up all the Mods and Rockers and attempting to march them out of town towards Rye, which gives them the opportunity to get a good look at everyone, so we need to avoid un-necessary attention. We need some kind of a diversion." Explained Steve.

Catch Us If You Can- The Dave Clark Five

With a white pillow case tied to his whip aerial Steve set off alone down the promenade past the Marina Building towards the Bathing Pool area in St. Leonards where he had been told that the Rockers could still be located.

All around Rockers watched with amusement as the lone Mod on his Vespa scooter weaved his way through the motorbikes, but none stopped him.

At the Bathing Pool, he dismounted looking strangely out of place in his parker surrounded by the leather clad motorcyclists.

"Does anyone here know where I can find any of the Southend on Sea Rockers."

"Why?" asked the large Rocker he recognised from the Evening Standard reporter incident on the beach and also his reddened nose which he gained through contact with Bandy Malc's head.

"I got a big problem and I need their help."

"I think this sorry shit has popped one too many of his funny pills or has some kind of death wish."

"Go and find any of the Southend Brothers and tell them we have a deluded Mod here asking for them."

Within minutes four motorcycles pulled into view and to Steve's relief Fred was astride one of them, together with Paul and his girlfriend on the pillion.

"Jesus, am I pleased to see you." Steve said as Fred dismounted and walked towards him.

"You know this idiot?"

"Known him since primary school, and he ain't an idiot. He used to be a biker but got led astray."

"Well he says that he needs your help."

"It's a long story, but that girl you saw me with the other day is the missing Russian diplomat's daughter that is spread over all the newspapers. I need to get her safely out of Hastings and with all the police activity I need some kind of diversion to get out of town without getting picked up. So, I thought if we could arrange some kind of a plan we could outfox the coppers."

"What do you need us to do?" asked Fred.

"A sort of an escort." Steve explained, "But I need your motorbike and leathers and some gear for the Russian bird and you take my scooter. The police are looking for a Mod and the missing girl on a scooter, the last place they are gonna look is at a Rocker and his bird on a motorbike."

Fred scratched his head, looked around him at the smiling faces and added, "I think we can arrange something like that eh lads?"

"It will be worth it just to see you riding a scooter in a parka." Smirked the large Rocker with a malicious grin on his face.

"To pull this off I will need one of your mate's girlfriend to lend her leather jacket and bone-dome. I promise she will get both back after we get out of town."

"So, when?"

"As soon as possible."

Steve gathered the group around him and told them of his plan.

"And the Rockers agreed?"

"Luckily Fred was there so I had one friend in the enemy camp,"

"Why would you do all this for me?" Nika asked

"For the moment, you are one of us and that's enough."

"But why would the Rockers help me. I thought the Mods and Rockers were enemies."

"They are just like us really, they just happen to prefer fast motorbikes and most of what you read in the news rags is crap designed to sell more papers.

Yeah there are few that are out looking for a bit of aggro but mostly it's just about getting away with your mates for a couple of days. Underneath that leather they have to go to work like the rest of us to earn a few bob. Any of us could just as easily become a Rocker, it's a way of expressing individuality."

"I'll ride with your mate Fred if you like. I am the same build, similar colour hair as Nika and wearing her clothes who could tell us apart on the back of a scooter?" said Razzle.

"And I have worked out a route for you to get out of town. Bexhill Road, De La Warr Road, follow the Bexhill Hospital signs, until you reach the A269 to Ninfield then continue on to Hailsham. Then from there it's up to you." Col added.

"Sounds good." asked Steve.

"But what do you plan for Nika then?" asked Razzle.

"It will be up to Nika to decide what she wants to do, but once out of Hastings it will give her more options." Declared Steve.

 Steve and Nika, Mike and Razzle flanked by Bandy Malc, Big Ron and Marshy set off towards the Bathing Pool, to meet up with the Rockers. If they got stopped by the police now all the planning would be in jeopardy.

As they passed the Masonic Hall just past the Marina building a Rocker rode up beside them and shouted there were cops at the Bo Peep pub so they needed to keep along the promenade as they approached the Bathing Pool area.

Fred was waiting for them as they brought their scooters to a halt with some thirty Rockers and their bikes waiting for them.

"This is Chrissy, Paul's girlfriend and she has agreed to lend Nika her leather jacket and crash helmet." Said Fred.

"She's a bit taller than me but it should fit OK." Chrissy noted but took off her jacket with some reluctance and handed it to the girl before her.

Nika put on the leathers and once her head was enclosed by the helmet she looked no different from any of the other Rocker birds.

As Steve and Fred swapped clothes a ripple of laughter and comments ran around the group, Fred now a Mod naturally receiving the majority of the ribald comments from his leather clad mates.

"Look after my scooter." Warned Steve as he helped Nika onto the back of the motorbike.

"I am more worried about you on something with more power than this souped-up hair dryer." Fred admitted.

"I'll look after it as if it were my own." Steve proclaimed.

"That's what worries me." Half-joked Fred.

"Now you know the plan, Fred here takes a hundred-yard lead then I swing in behind him with the other Rockers, the scooters then bringing up the rear-guard and block anything following us. Once we get to Bexhill Old Town and turn off for the hospital, Fred and Razzle carry on towards Little Common and Eastbourne as a decoy, just in case we are followed. The Rockers stay with me riding shotgun until we all meet up at Hailsham at the church."

Bandy Malc keeps the scooters back in case we run into trouble. All clear?"

"Let's do it." Shouted Fred as he gunned the Vespa with full throttle towards the Bexhill Road.

Steve felt the throb of the 500cc engine beneath him as he twisted the throttle, gave it a few more seconds, slipped it into first gear and accelerated away feeling Nika's arms gripping him tightly around his waist.

To any bystanders, it was a hapless Mod being pursued by a gang of Rockers and the type of hooligan action they would expect from the youngsters.

Steve kept the distance behind Fred, but had to throttle back to ensure he did not catch up to him too quickly. Behind him the Rockers maintained position.

All went to plan and when Steve reached Bexhill Old Town he turned off to the right following the sign to the hospital, all was going to plan.

Once clear of Bexhill Steve opened up the BSA 500, bringing back a sense of speed he had not felt for a while on his Vespa and he had to admit it felt good.

It's All Over Now – The Rolling Stones

Steve lit a cigarette and sat on the low wall by the church where he had planned for everyone to meet up.

He now waited for the scooters to turn up and it was with relief when his red Sportique turned up in one piece with Razzle on the back, followed shortly by the others.

"Rozzers stopped us in Little Common." Explained Fred with a broad smile on his face, "But Razzle here soon persuaded them that she was not a Russian with some pretty colourful Anglo-Saxon expletives."

Steve turned to Nika and noticed she had that faraway look in her eyes, "You alright?"

"I've decided that I am going to hand myself in at the police station, so I think you and your friends had better make yourself scarce."

"I'll make up some story about getting a lift from a guy who thought I was a hitch hiker and then tried to get a bit amorous running his hand up my thigh, so he pushed me out of the car when I didn't respond to his advances and found myself lost in the middle of nowhere until I ended up here."

"Will your father believe that story?" Steve inquired.

"Would his little girl lie? Having to live rough and being frightened and alone in a strange country, plus a few tears. It will work. Look at my shoes scuffed and soiled, and wearing clothes I stole from a washing line."

"You are terrible."

Nika smiled and reached into her handbag, "And I want you to take this, so you can buy everyone here a drink for all of their help."

Steve looked at the wad of notes and whistled, "There must be a hundred quid here, I can't take that, that's more than fifteen week's wages."

"It was worth it. I have never had so much fun until I met you and your friends. It just a way of saying thanks."

"I don't want your money. I just want to know that you will be OK."

"Take it. My father wouldn't even miss it."

"Here I have written my address, write to me if you can." Said Steve handing her a scrap of paper.

"Walk me to the nearest police station, then get on your way back to Southend with your friends."

Steve watched as Nika pushed open the door of the police station, she turned and briefly smiled then went inside.

The group had waited for Steve's return and stood smoking by the churchyard.

"So, she handed herself in?" Razzle asked.

"Yes, just walked straight in."

"What happened?"

"I dunno I didn't hang around."

"Do you think she will be alright?"

"She concocted a story which sounded as though she had been picked up by a bloke who tried to grope her, and dumped her by the roadside when she didn't cooperate leaving her totally lost, frightened and disorientated."

"Might work, "Said Razzle.

"Well if the copper's come knocking on my door I'll know it didn't wash."

Walking round the group Steve handed out fivers to all those who had helped with the escapade, "It is a thank you from Nika, it is her way of saying thanks."

The sudden appearance of a policeman gave Steve a moment of panic.

"Alright you lot move on, we don't want any trouble, here do we?"

"We ain't causing any trouble" Bandy Malc responded.

"Al the same I want you to move on."

"Right officer."

Returning to their motorbikes and scooters the group split up to go their separate ways. Fred pleased to be back in his leathers and to have the power of his bike back again rather than the souped-up Singer sewing machine he had elected to ride here, kick started his BSA into life and headed off with the other Rockers.

The Southend Mods group did a couple of circuits of the car park just to piss off the copper before setting off.

The policeman just stood and watched convincing himself that he had successfully defused a serious situation from developing between these warring gangs.

It's Over-Roy Orbison

In the days following the so called 'Second Battle of Hastings' the newspapers were full of headlines:
ARRESTS REACH 70 AFTER HASTINGS CLASHES.

POLICE MARCH GANG'S OUT TO TOWN BOUNDARIES.

The papers also carried accounts of Bank Holiday Weekend.

HASTINGS August 3
Police here went on the offensive this evening to clear the town and seafront of hordes of youths who had spent the weekend fighting and terrorizing holidaymakers.
Using completely new tactics, they horded the Mods and Rockers and their followers into groups of 75 to 500 and marched them three miles to the borough boundaries.
Most of the groups departed readily, as they have become so used to marching sheepishly behind their leaders that few realised what was happening until they were well on the way to Rye.
Youths attempting to get back into town by public transport were taken off the buses and allowed back in small groups on foot.

But the headline that caught Steve's eye was the one he had been looking for:
RUSSIAN DIPLOMAT'S DAUGHTER FOUND.
Nika Petrov, the daughter of the Russian diplomat Alexandre Petrov walked into Hailsham Police Station after having being abducted while holidaying in Kent.
Her abductor, a middle-aged man after unsuccessfully trying to molest her threw her out of the car we believe near the Ashdown Forest where alone and frightened she wandered for two days too afraid to approach anybody to help her in this country that was so foreign to her. She apologised for stealing clothes off of a washing line when hers became torn and dirty.
Her mother and father were overjoyed at their daughters return.
The Police are asking for any information concerning a green Austin A35 that the victim described as her abductor's vehicle on Saturday 1st August, in or around the Hawkhurst/Flimwell area.
Initial reports that she was seen on a scooter have been discounted as coincidence.

Steve smiled to himself, she had done exactly as she said she would and had protected Steve and his friends, their escape plan had worked.

A few weeks later a foreign postcard dropped onto the front door mat at Steve's home, a picture of the Kremlin and on the reverse the simple message 'From Russia With Love'.

The Summer Of '64 (Stu's Story)

Clacton during Easter Bank Holiday in 1964 had been the coldest on record for over 100 years and a thoroughly dismal weekend but now as Whitsun approached the weather had improved and the Mods were all waiting to find out which would be the next seaside town to be invaded.

For one of the original Hasting's Mods, Stu Barnes the forthcoming weekend was to change his life in more ways than one and turn his world upside down.

No Particular Place To Go-Chuck Berry

John Piddock walked out of his office, looked at his watch before going into the back of the garage he managed and watched his two mechanics at work, "Pull your collective fingers out, both these cars have got to be finished by twelve thirty."
Paul looked up from the Ford Anglia 105E he was working on and gave John the thumbs up, "Practically finished Boss."
"Just the plugs and points and this little Mk 1 frog-eyed Sprite will be finished." Responded Stu, a big grin on his face.
"Good, well make sure both cars are completed and put outside in the yard for collection." John said as he made his way back to his office.
"He don't look like he has the Bank Holiday spirit, does he?" commented Paul.
"The idea of paying us for a day off goes against the grain with him and with all the pressures of owning this place on his shoulders, you can't blame him."
After driving the two cars out into the client collection area, and having swept up the workshop it was time to close up. After cleaning their hands with Swarfega and peeling off their overalls, the two put on their respective clothes, Paul a leather jacket and Stu his fur trimmed Parka and walked towards their mounts.
"Can't see why you bother with that souped-up hair dryer." laughed Paul as he mounted his Triumph Bonneville.
"This Vespa GS 160 is the bee's knees, neat and a real bird puller, unlike that mobile oil slick on wheels."
"Yeah but it'll do over a ton, 650cc's, 46 break horsepower, probably the best motorbike in the world." Boasted Paul.
"Speed ain't everything." Declared Stu.
"Total Bollocks, speed gets the old adrenaline pumping, and nothing beats the feeling of the wind in your face as you twist the old throttle and hear the engine revving to the limit as you hit one hundred miles an hour."
"So, what you doing Bank Holiday Monday?" Stu asked.
"Dunno yet, depends on what the rest of the lads have got planned."
"Word is it could be Margate or Brighton."
"Prefer Brighton, as Margate is a bit of a shit hole, hopefully all you Mods will go to Margate and stay out of our way." And with that he kicked the Bonnie into life and pulled off leaving Stu sitting astride his Vespa deep in thought. Easter had been a disaster, bloody cold, wet and the whole place was fucking closed, but the newspapers made it sound like the Third World War with headlines like 'Wild Ones Invade Seaside, 97 arrested'. It was the first time that Mods had outnumbered the Rockers but in reality, everyone was too bloody frozen to cause anybody much grief, which just left the heavy-handed approach of the coppers trying to separate them and causing more trouble than the two groups had actually been involved in.
Stu and a few of the Hastings Mods had made to trek up to Clacton and swore in future to stay this side of the Thames. The East London Mods were fucking head cases and thought they were the dog's bollocks, fighting with anybody be they Mods or Rockers. Hopefully this weekend would be better.

"So?" demanded Stu as he sat round the table in the Pam Dor with the usual Saturday night crowd, "Margate or Brighton?"

Col pushed his empty Pyrex cup around in front of him, "Well Margate is about 70 miles away and Brighton is only half that from here in Hastings, so I say Brighton."

"Yeah, Brighton." Bob added

Stu looked across at the next table and asked Lloyd who considered himself an Ace Face, "Brighton has the better clubs for dancing."

Bob looked up after carefully considering the question, "At Easter we all went to fucking Clacton and what happened the fucking Rockers turned up here while we were freezing our nuts off up there, so maybe we should just stay put."

"But all the signs are it's gonna be down here, either Brighton or Margate." Stu remonstrated.

"OK, Brighton." Col declared, "Now let's get another coffee in and put something decent on that juke box."

"So, we go tomorrow morning?" Stu asked.

"Might as well, fuck all else to do." Bob added.

"Never know we might meet up with some nice birds." Col said with a smile on his face before he realised that Linda his current girlfriend had arrived and was standing behind him.

"And you think you are leaving us at home while you go off galivanting about?" Linda questioned, the menace evident in her voice.

"Obviously I meant Bob and Stu might meet up with some nice birds." Remarked Col trying to dig himself out of the hole that he had dug for himself.

"So, you are taking me with you?" Linda asked sounding more like a statement than a question.

"How could I leave you at home." Col said the resignation clear in his voice.

"Then that's settled." Linda stated.

Stu could not help but laugh at his friend's situation, one that for him was not a problem at the moment being foot loose and bird free, and as Col had said there might be some decent birds over in Brighton, but not too decent he hoped.

"Anyone got any uppers?" Bob demanded, "Might need some over the next day or two."

"Think we might have to go down to the Pump House and see what's available, bound to be someone with some Hearts for sale." Stu concluded.

Hubble Bubble (Toil and Trouble)- Manfred Mann

It was nearly midday before the friends met up at Warrior Square, St Leonards on Sea. Stu turned up first shortly followed by Col and Linda and Bob arrived late as usual.

"You'll be fucking late for your own funeral." Col said impatiently, stubbing out another cigarette.

"Had a bit of trouble stating my scooter." Bob said lamely.

"Fucking Lambretta's are too fucking temperamental, you ought to get yourself a Vespa."

"My LI 150 is faster than your Vespa." Bob responded.

"You must be joking the LI tops out at fifty-three MPH, while the GS is nearly ten MPH quicker." Stu reminded his friend.

"Well the guy I brought it from said it was a real goer."

"Yeah if the fucking thing starts at all." Laughed Stu, "Come on let's get a move on. We'll go via Hailsham and Lewes to miss the traffic on the coast road, it'll be quicker."

Turning right at the traffic lights on the seafront they headed up London Road to Silverhill, then followed Battle Road out of St Leonards towards Battle.

By the time they reached Hailsham the little convoy had gained another half dozen Mods and as they approached Lewes the group had grown to sixteen scooters. It would seem they were not alone in heading to Brighton.

From Lewes the A27 was a constant stream of scooters as they accelerated their way down the Lewes Road towards the seafront, it felt to Stu as if they were part of an unstoppable movement.

Moving forward on his seat, knees against the leg shield, leaning forward Stu struck the Mod pose as he gunned the GS through the traffic, a broad smile spread across his face as Col and Bob followed him. A few policemen stood helpless as the volume of youngsters on their scooters roared passed them, shouting and declaring their presence, laughter and the sound of revving engines demonstrating to the world that they had arrived.

On the seafront there was not hundreds but thousands of Parka-clad Mods as the trio looked for somewhere to park in the hazy sunshine reflecting of off the sea.

"Fuck me." Declared Col as he looked around. "Must be all the South London Mods have descended on the town."

"And a fair number of North London Mods as well by the look of the cut of their suits." Remarked Stu, who had the eye for the latest fashion trends.

"I only hope the East London Mods have gone to Margate, everybody hates those bastards, and they hate everybody else be they Mods or Rockers."

Linda was aware that Mod girls were in the minority, and in retrospect she should have stayed at home and gone shopping and let the lads have some fun.

"So where are the Rockers?" Bob demanded in a loud voice.

A Mod with 'Chelsea' in white letters on his Parka turned and pointed further along the beach where a line of policemen was trying to keep a small number of Rockers out of the clutches of countless Mods on the beach and added, "We must outnumber them one 'undred to one, the poor bastards don't stand a chance."

Stu looked across the pebble beach, holiday makers, kids and oldies were making the most of the fine weather, some even braving the sea for a swim.

"ain't like Clacton Eh?" Stu added.

"That was the pits. Whose idea was it to have a Bank Holiday in April?" Bob demanded.

"Because it was fucking Easter you moron, that's why." Linda explained.

"But why do they close the banks?" Bob asked.

Linda shut her eyes and slowly shook her head and suspected that although the lights were on, there was nobody home in his thick skull.

"Come on let's go down on the beach, that's where all the action is." Stu suggested.

Threading their way down onto the stony beach was a job in itself, the staircase was packed with Mods and holidaymakers either making for the beach or leaving it.

"Come on let's go for a paddle." Suggested Stu as he made his way down to the water's edge.

"Are you fucking mad?" Col interjected.

"Why not? it's traditional to have a dip in the sea during the Bank Holiday weekend."

"All you need is a knotted hanky on yer head to really fit in." Sniggered Col.

"When I was a nipper me mum and dad took me to the beach during the holidays, it was the thing to do, so it just seems natural." Stu reminisced.

"My God if it ain't Stuart Barnes as I live and breathe."

Stu turned to see his old friend from school who had moved to Brighton a year or so ago, "Sid. What the fuck are you doing here?"

"Same as you by the look of it. Don't know if you have met Annie?"

Stu turned and looked at Sid's girlfriend, a pretty little thing with glasses and a winning smile, "Pleased to meet you, but God knows what you see in this reprobate?"

"He told me he was good with his hands." She giggled.

"What Desert Disease? Wandering Palms?" Col added with a sly wink.

"No, I met him at the Bus garage on the Lewis Road, I was working in the office and he was in the engine department and he repaired my old scooter in between fixing the buses."

"Wow a bird with her own scooter, a real modette." Linda declared.

All heads turned towards the sea at the sound of screaming, nobody seemed to move as it became obvious that a girl was in some kind of trouble.

Without thinking twice Stu chucked off his Parka and desert boots and run into the surf. The girl was about fifteen feet out but obviously in distress, and as Stu neared he could see the red colouration of the water around her and shouted to her that he was coming.

"It's alright darling I'll get you." Stu shouted as the girl turned to face him, her long black hair hung limply to her face and her mascara had run, looking like black tears streaming down her face "I think something has happened to my foot, it hurts real bad." She sobbed.

"Don't worry I'll get you back to the beach." Stu said as firmly as he could.

With her arms wrapped about his neck he made his way back into the shallower water before finally getting her back onto the shingle.

Annie and Linda rushed forward and it was obvious that she had cut her foot badly.

"Gonna need stitches." Annie proclaimed, "We need to get her to casualty."

"Where are your clothes?" Linda asked.

"Just over there." The girl answered, pointing to a pile of clothes not more than six feet away.

By now a small crowd had gathered around and Stu looked up helplessly, wondering what he should do.

"Keep her leg elevated," suggested one of the onlookers, "and put a bandage around her foot tightly to try and stop the bleeding."

For the first time he looked properly at the girl and behind the dishevelled wet hair and smudged makeup, it was her eyes that caught his attention, deep brown and they were staring straight at him.

"What's your name?" she asked softly

"Stuart, but everybody calls me Stu."

Before he could say anything else, Linda returned with a towel and a selection of clothes.

"She's a Rocker." Linda said with distaste holding up a leather skirt and tasselled leather jacket, "A fucking Rocker."

"She's hurt." Stu stated, "And I don't give a flying fuck what she is."

With her arms around Sid and Stu's shoulders after she had dressed with aid from the girls, they half carried her up the beach towards the steps up onto the promenade back to where Stu had parked his scooter.

For the first time Stu realised he was saturated as well, his jeans clinging to his legs, his new Fred Perry shirt bloodied.

"I'm sorry." the girl whispered as she watched him looking down at his wet and stained clothes.

"Don't worry lass, I'll dry out."

I Want To Hold Your Hand- The Beatles

With help from Sid and Annie the girl was lifted onto the pillion seat of Stu's GS, his Parka around her shoulders for the short drive up to the local Casualty Department. Bob, Col and Linda formed up beside him.

"I'll go in with her." Stu said, as he helped her off his scooter.

"We'll wait for you." Linda added.

"You go back to the beach, I'll try and find you later, I've no idea how long I will be."

"We will wait for you near the pier." Bob suggested.

"OK."

With his arm around the girl they entered into the busy casualty department which looked more like a war zone than a British hospital, red faced holiday makers who had had too much sun, a number of Mods and Rockers with assorted injuries and numerous other sick looking people waiting to be attended to, the place was packed.

"Name?" the receptionist asked as they reached the admittance desk.

For the first time Stu realised he had no idea of the girl's name, in all the excitement he had never asked her.

"Surname? The woman demanded.

"Phillips."

"Christian name?"

"Sandra."

Date of Birth?"

"Sixth of June, forty-seven."

"Address?"

"Fifty-one Wickham Avenue, Bexhill on Sea."

"GP's name?"

"Dr Davey, 24 Albert Road, Bexhill"

"Nature of visit?"

"I cut my foot badly." The girl named Sandra replied.

"Go and take a seat and wait for your name to be called." The receptionist said mechanically.

As they took their seats it was obvious from the looks of those around them that the combination of a Rocker bird and a Mod was causing some consternation to the other patients especially one tall Rocker who got up and walked across to them, "You alright darling? Has this little sod hurt you?"

Sandra looked up, anger across her face, "Hurt me? No, he fucking well helped me when I must have stood on a bottle or something and cut my foot. And where were you fucking lot? standing behind a fucking line of coppers like sheep."

"We woz outnumbered." The Rocker answered sheepishly, and I got hit by a stone on my head."

"Lucky it hit you where it could do little harm." Sandra said with more than a hint of sarcasm.

Stu watched as the Rocker returned to his seat, "Thanks that could have turned nasty. Do you want me to wait with you?"

"Only if you want to. When I get through here I would have to make my way back to the railway station to get a train back home."

"I'll take you home on my scooter. No problem. You shouldn't be walking on that foot."

"You live around here" Sandra asked.

"No. Live in Hastings so it's on my way home."

"But don't you want to get back to your friends?

"They will be alright."

Sandra put her hand on Stu's knee and smiled, "I never said thank you to you and your friends for helping me. You didn't need to go to all this trouble."

"How could I leave a damsel in distress?" Stu replied.

"Even though I am a Rocker?"

"Couldn't tell that when you were just in that swimming costume, even so it's a long time since I have had a beautiful girl on the back of me scooter."

Sandra blushed and leant forward and kissed Stu on the cheek.

It was some three hours later that Sandra foot bandaged after nine stitches climbed onto the pillion seat of Stu's Vespa and set off towards Bexhill.

Stu felt strangely contented with Sandra's arms wrapped about his waist as he gunned the 160cc to full power.

Not Fade Away- The Rolling Stones

It was late as Stu pulled into the side alley of his parent's house to park up his scooter for the night. At first, he had thought to go back to Brighton after dropping off Sandra in Bexhill. Her father had been worried when a scruffy Mod had brought back his daughter, with her foot bandaged and obviously still in pain, but had welcomed him in when she had explained the situation.

Now as he walked in the back door of his home he was confronted by his father, who had a look of thunder on his face, "Look at the fucking state of you, blood soaked clothes and looked bloody dishevelled. Been fighting have you with your tearaway friends at some seaside resort? Yes, I have heard the radio, Mods rampaging through the streets of Brighton, knocking over old ladies and frightening poor holiday makers."

"It wasn't like that and no I have not been fighting."

"Then explain those." His father said pointing at the blood stains on his jeans and Fred Perry shirt.

"It's a long story but I helped a girl who had been injured and had cut her foot, took her to casualty then took her home." Stu explained.

"Yeah, and pigs might fly." retorted his father in disbelief.

"Well it's fucking true." Stu answered defiantly.

"You know your mother is worried sick when you go off on one of these weekends, always fearing the worse that you may get hurt."

"The press exaggerates what is going on, yes there is some violence but no more than any football match on any Saturday night."

"That's as may be, but you can't deny everything that is in the papers, after Clacton they said there were over ninety arrests for vandalism and that was not the press saying that but what happened in the courts."

"I'm tired and I am going to bed and get out of these damp clothes." Stu said finally, before leaving his father standing there.

The next morning Stu studied his Vespa and the blood stains on the rear bubble and running board and his thoughts turned back to the previous day

He had not been able to get the memory of yesterday out of his mind and in particular the girl Sandra. Yes, she was a Rocker and that in itself was a problem, but if he was true to himself she had had quite an effect on him.

Mod blokes did not usually go for Rocker birds, that was a big no-no and he could already imagine what Linda and her friends would say if he let his true feelings be known.

He should go back to Brighton to meet up if he could with his friends, but he knew that he had to see Sandra again and to see if she was alright, so after cleaning off he scooter he headed back to Bexhill.

The house was larger than he remembered it from last night and what was more worrying was the BSA Gold Star parked in the front garden. Was it her boyfriend's machine?"

He rang the front door bell and waited.

The door opened and a young guy obviously a Rocker with greased back hair looked at Stu, then towards the scooter parked in the road.

"I just wondered if I could have a word with Sandra?"

"Hey Sis there's some scrawny little Mod here either deluded or lost who wants to talk to you."

"Is it Stuart?" came a voice from the front room.

Stu nodded.

"Yep it appears it is."

"Then let him in."

"You had better go in." Sandra's brother said as he moved to one side to let him pass.

Sandra was sitting on the settee with her bandaged foot up resting on a cushion when Stu walked into the front room.

"How are you today?" Stu asked awkwardly.

"Like my foot is on fire and still hurts like hell, but it was so kind of you to bring me home."

"It was the least I could do."

"Jim this is Stu he was the one who brought home last night."

Stu turned towards Jim whose attitude had changed since he opened the door, "And you let him bring you back on that souped-up sewing machine parked out there."

"I would have had to come back on the train but he offered to give me a ride to my door."

"I hate to say this to a Mod, but thanks for looking after my little sister."

"She could hardly walk so how could I just let her walk to the station to catch a train?"

"There must have been some other Rockers around who could have helped."

"Well there wasn't, so Stu offered or rather insisted that he brought me home."

"Is that your DBD34 outside? Stu asked.

"You know about bikes?"

"Didn't always ride a Vespa. Had a couple of motorbikes myself before turning Mod. Is it one of the later models with the very high first gear, enabling you to get up to sixty before changing up to second?"

"Hey this Mod knows his bikes, Yep and it has the 38mm bell-mouth Amal carb and swept back exhaust and will top out at about 110mph."

"My mate Paul at work would give you a run for your money with his 650 Bonnie."

"The only Paul I know is Paul Stevens who has a Bonnie."

"That's him."

"You work with him?"

"Yeah we are both mechanics at Winchelsea Road Garage in Ore."

"Shit, Paul is a mate of mine, said once he worked with an alright Mod but no-one believed him."

Sandra tutted very loudly to ensure she was heard, then added," I think Stu here came to see how I was not to get into some lengthy discussion on motorbikes."

Just One Look- The Hollies

It was Friday night and Stu made his way up the steep staircase into the Pam Dor which as usual with filled with cigarette smoke while the juke box vied for attention above the hub-dub of voices.

"Where the fuck have you been?" Col demanded as he reached the table occupied by his friends.

"Been working."

"No, I meant where the fuck did you get to last weekend, we waited and you never came back."

"Ended up waiting in casualty for ages then I took the girl home to Bexhill."

"You took that Rocker bird home on your scooter?" demanded Linda.

"Well she could hardly walk anywhere, could she?"

"Didn't take you as a Rocker lover." Sneered Bob.

"Probably spread her legs to say thank you." Linda said with venom.

"It was nothing like that, I just felt sorry for her and I would have done the same for any of you."

"But she was a Rocker."

"She in fact has a name, Sandra, and she was quiet badly cut and had to have nine stiches and her foot bandaged up by the nurses."

"So?" demanded Linda.

"So, I took her home, end of story."

"But you never came back." Said Col.

"Did I miss anything?" asked Stu.

"A few bundles with the Rockers, deck chairs at fifty paces and a lot of running about but nothing much else. The Rockers were so outnumbered I think most of them went home and left us in control of the seafront."

"Don't sound like I missed much then." Admitted Stu who was becoming tired of the conversation.

"It was being there that was important, part of the whole Mod thing, solidarity, a sense of being." Bob said.

"And I thought it was the music, Tamala Motown, Ska, our clothes and our scooters that defined us as Mods. We didn't become Mods to fight Rockers, as we have coexisted here in Hastings for years without any serious problems, so why is that so important now?"

"We are the new generation; the Rockers live in the past with their Rock 'n Roll music and the way they dress in fucking leathers." Explained Col.

"The only reason they wear leather for riding their bikes is because if or when you have a crash or fall off it provides better protection and saves your skin from abrasion."

"Meeting one Rocker bird and he is now defending them." Linda added.

"I rode motorbikes and wore leathers before Mods ever existed. It was my choice to change, the Rockers just preferred to continue with their bikes and their way of life and that was their choice."

"Anybody would think you were supporting them?" Bob stated.

"I work with a Rocker and he is an OK kind of a guy, not that much different from you and me, chases women, enjoys a drink and lives for his motorbike."

"Sounds to me like you are losing the plot." Concluded Col.

Stu just stopped before responding and realised what he must have sounded like to his friends, but then it struck him that yes, maybe he had changed, but then that was not the first time this week he had had that sensation.

"So, when was you gonna tell me you met me mate Jim?" Paul asked as they had their coffee break.
"Jim?"
"Yeah Jim Phillips."
"Oh, that Jim."
"He told me what you had done for his sister at the weekend and was pretty impressed even though you were a fucking Mod."
"I only took her home." Stu said defensively.
"Well his sister said that you had gone into the sea to save her and then had taken her to hospital, before you took her all the way home." Paul paused before continuing, "On your bloody scooter."
Stu looked down at the cigarette he was holding, too embarrassed to look his friend in the eye.
"Well it seems his little sister has taken quiet a shine to you, even though you are a bloody Mod."
"I didn't know she was a Rocker when I pulled her out of the sea, she was wearing a swimsuit."
"Would that have made any difference?"
"No, I just saw a girl in trouble. But it didn't go down that well with my friends."
"The fact that she is a bit of alright didn't influence you?"
"It was only when I got her to the beach that I noticed that she was pretty damn beautiful."
"So, you fancy her?"
"I dunno, me being a Mod and her a Rocker certainly adds a complication."
"So, what you gonna do about it?"
"I want to see her again but I can't see it going anywhere. My friends will never accept her and the Rockers certainly won't accept me."
"There comes a time when you have to make a choice, and if you really like her I am sure you will think of something."

World Without Love- Peter and Gordon

It had been a couple of years since Stu had looked at his old motorbike that he had kept covered up in the garden shed. It was the machine that he had rebuilt and modified from the ground up and had helped him decide that he wanted to be a mechanic, but he had kept the bike rather than selling it when he had had his hair cut and brought his first scooter and took on the role of a Mod.

Pulling the dust sheet back Stu studied the bike he knew every inch of. It was a 1957 AJS Model 20, 485cc OHV twin, black frame and tank with chromed sides to the petrol tank.

It was not as fast as the modern bikes but to Stu's eyes it was a classic and he had a yearning now to see if it still ran.

First, he had to charge up the battery, check the plugs and chain tension.

Hanging on the back of the door was his old leather jacket and on the shelf his crash helmet, only ever worn to keep your head warm in the winter.

Stu smiled to himself as he polished the paintwork and wondered what his friends would think if they could see him now.

It was late evening, dusk when he kick-started the AJS, bringing it back to life.

Donning his leather jacket and wrapping a silk scarf round his face and putting on his helmet he reckoned nobody could possible recognise him and he set off towards Bexhill.

Along the De La Warr Road he passed about four scooters who paid him scant interest apart from a bit of verbal abuse as he gunned the throttle easily passing them. He had to admit to himself that it was good to have the power and acceleration between his legs again.

If the first visit to Sandra's house had elicited a scowl from her brother, this time the look he got was one of total shock as he pulled off his helmet.

"Sis there's some Rocker here wants to see you." Jim called upstairs.

"Who is it?" came the response.

"Come and see."

"I'm not in the mood to see anybody." Sandra called down.

"You will want to see this one." Jim laughed.

Slowly Sandra edged down the stairs trying not to put any weight on her injured foot and then as she reached the bottom stood, her mouth dropping open at the sight off the mysterious Rocker before her, "Stu?"

"Seems like the boy has seen the light." smirked Jim as he walked down the path to look at the AJS.

"But......." Sandra started to say but words failed her.

"Just thought I would take my old bike out for a spin and could not think of anywhere better to go than to see if you were alright."

"But you are a Mod?"

"I wasn't always."

"I don't understand." Sandra said still confused by the whole situation.

"I just wanted to see you again."

Sandra stepped forward and pulled his head down and kissed him full on the lips, her tongue exploring his mouth as she pressed herself against his body.

"Do you wanna go for a spin on me bike?" Stu finally manged to ask as Sandra stepped back.

"Where shall we go?"

"I thought about going over to see Sid and Annie, the couple that helped us on the beach."

"What will they think about seeing you with me?"

"I've known Sid for years, like me he cares more about engines and motors and I am sure he would want to know that you are OK, and won't give a toss whether I arrive on a scooter or a motorbike."

"Nice bike, looks in pretty good nick." Jim said as he returned from giving the AJS a once over.

"Did all the modifications myself, rebuilt the engine and always had a soft spot for that model, probably why I didn't get rid of it. Not as fast as your bike but still good for 90mph."

"Stu's taking me out for a spin so keep him occupied while I go get myself ready."

"And who is this?" came a voice from the kitchen.

Jim turned and introduced his father and added, "This is the young man who brought Sandra back from Brighton."

"I know, just didn't recognise him in leathers, Don't I know you?" Sandra's father asked.

Stu shook his head, excepting for when he brought Sandra home.

"You work at Piddock's garage, don't you?"

"Yeah I'm one of the mechanics up there."

"Then you have probably worked on my car."

"What do you drive?"

"Austin-Healey Mk.1 Sprite."

"Not the one I worked on a week ago?"

"Yes, the light blue Frog-eye."

"You did the service?"

"Yes."

"Well you did a good job on it, drives like a dream."

"We aim to please."

"John Piddock and I went to school together and I know he takes pride in the work done in his workshop, and if he trusts you that is good enough for me."

"Then you do not mind if I take your daughter out for a ride?"

"If you don't treat her right I know where to find you." He said, with a knowing smile spread across his face.

"He must have something as she has been really moody since she saw him last, and this is a side of my little sister that I have never seen before, I think she really likes him." Jim added.

"Are you talking about me?" Sandra demanded as she came back downstairs.

"As if we would." Jim said turning to his father with a conspiratorial wink.

"Come on let's go before they start showing you pictures of me when I was a baby and embarrassing me." Said Sandra.

Tell Me When- The Applejacks

Stu felt like he was living a double life, riding his scooter then incognito on his AJS. In truth he enjoyed both, each was different and satisfying, but was he being true to himself and others? What would his Mod friends think of him in leathers astride a motorbike and would he still be able to see Sandra if he were a Mod?

The answer could well be resolved when he passed his driving test later this week. He had learned to drive working in the garage but he had booked three driving lessons with BSM in an Austin A40 Farina as he had been told that he stood more chance of passing if he turned up in an established driving school car.

Now he studied his Highway Code but his mind kept drifting back to Sandra. He had never met a girl like her and now she was back to full health he found himself wanting to spend more time with her.

The fact she had her own motorbike, a 200cc Tiger Cub had come as a surprise and she rode it like a maniac. Encased in leather jacket and tight leather trousers she was fearless on the road and equally fearless on the back of his AJS, and looked good.

Sid and Annie had been more than pleased to see them together and Sandra seemed to really get on with Annie and over the ensuing weeks had spent more time going over to Brighton to see them, a sort of neutral territory where they were less likely to be recognised.

The conversation often went back to the Whitsun weekend and Annie eventually found out why she was on the beach alone."

"Well I went with two friends on the train so we could all be together, but they got chatted up and left me alone on that beach. With all that was going on I thought I might as well have a swim before going home alone. A couple of boys tried to chat me up but it was obvious that their intent was to get in my knickers, so I told them to fuck off."

"So how much of a surprise was it when Stu came charging into the sea."

"I didn't even see him at first, I was hurting really badly when I had stepped on something really sharp and the pain was terrible and blood everywhere and I started screaming. Then there was this bloke wrapping his arms around me and telling me I would be OK as he carried me to the beach."

"The silly sod ran in fully clothed, without thinking twice." Said Annie.

"It was only when he lay me on the stones that I even looked at him and to my horror I realised he was a Mod."

"Did that matter to you?" Annie inquired.

Sandra laughed, "Thought they were all pounces, dressed up in their fine clothes and Parka's and riding pissy little scooters and the Mod girls were even worse, stuck up little bitches."

"But what did you think of Stu?"

"I didn't know what to make of him and felt a bit uncomfortable when we went into the casualty department but he just stayed regardless of the looks he was getting from the assorted Mods and Rockers waiting to get patched up, and he sat and waited until they had stitched my foot then offered me a lift home on his fucking scooter, but how could I say I'm not getting on that, so I didn't, and climbed on as I could not face walking back to the station and waiting for a train."

"But you seem to be getting on now?"

"Never felt this way about a bloke before and when he turned up on a bike you could have knocked me over with a feather, I was truly gobsmacked."

"He and Sid used to tinker about on bikes for hours when they both lived in Hastings, a real couple of tearaways." Annie added.

"I can imagine that. It's obvious he thinks a lot of you both and I know he feels comfortable here. I still think he is torn between being a Mod and having a Rocker girlfriend, but that is a decision that he will have to make."

"What would happen if he decided to remain a Mod?" Annie asked interested to hear Sandra's response.

Sandra thought before answering, Annie could see it was a difficult problem for the girl, "Then I would have to do something about it, so would you come shopping with me if I came over to Brighton next Saturday morning because I am going to need some help choosing the right gear?"

Can't You See That She Is Mine- The Dave Clark Five

Stu nearly had a heart attack when he saw who his examiner was, 'Failure' Fowler himself, looking less than happy to be going out on this damp June morning.

"Read that number plate." He demanded, which Stu duly did before getting in the car and adjusting his rear-view mirror as the instructor had told him.

The route followed a well-rehearsed route, down London Road, Norman Road then turning onto the seafront and turning up Harley Shute Road at the traffic lights. With the emergency stop and three-point turn out of the way he returned to the Test Centre and answered a few questions on the Highway Code.

"Well Mr Barnes you have passed your driving test and handed him his pass certificate and left the car.

Stu would now be able to road test cars up at the garage, legally, as he had been doing it for some time already and more importantly he could get himself some wheels, four wheels that is.

The little lock-up garage in Western Road was his next stop where he had seen a Morris minivan with a quite few miles on the clock but within his price range.

"Just one owner, nice little runner." George the proprietor said as he patted the bonnet.

"Who was that the British Army?" joked Stu and he noted the two-tone paint job, red and primer, plus numerous bumps and scratches.

"How many miles on the clock before you rewound it?" Stu asked sarcastically.

George looked at him, his eyebrow raised, "As if I would do such a thing."

"Well I reckon she has at least fifty thousand miles on her, looking at the wear on the accelerate pedal and threadbare carpet, and the moss growing in the slide window runners"

"You some kind of expert?" George asked.

"Should be I work up at Winchelsea Road Garage as a mechanic, so cut the crap and give me your best price."

"Well maybe it is a bit rough around the edges but the engine is good and the sub-frames are OK."

"Well start it up and if I see a big cloud of white smoke I am walking away."

Much to Stu's surprise the motor turned over first time and sounded good.

"OK you got a deal. I need to arrange some finances and insurance and I will be back tomorrow to pick it up and I want it still to have this same engine in it."

"You really know how to hurt an honest salesman, questioning my integrity."

"I learnt everything from my boss John Piddock and when I told him I had seen a motor here he warned me about you."

"And I thought John was my friend." George said shaking his head, but smiling broadly.

Putting in a bit of unpaid overtime Stu gave the Mini the once over, new plugs and points, new air and oil filters, oil change and sprayed the subframes with flushing oil to prevent them rusting, and now he was going to drive over to Bexhill to show it off to Sandra who at first thought he was mad to switch to four wheels when he had a perfectly good motorbike and that souped-up hair dryer called a Vespa.

But now as he rang the front door bell he hoped she would be pleased with his purchase, because now they could go anywhere without being wrapped up in Parka's or leathers against the elements.

Sandra's dad opened the door and smiled as he spotted the minivan parked out front and called upstairs for his daughter., "Come on Sandra your carriage awaits."

Jim wandered into the hall and nodded, then turned as he heard his sister coming down the stairs.

If Sandra had been shocked when Stu turned up in leathers it was nothing to what appeared at the top of the stairs. Her dad, Jim and Stu just watched as this apparition of beauty appeared before them, short above knee black dress that only emphasised her slim figure, long straightened dark brown hair that framed her face and curled in under her chin and black eyeliner that seemed to enhance her big brown eyes.

"Sorry young lady, can you send my tomboy sister down, her boyfriend is here,"

Turning her face towards Jim she screwed up her face and stuck her tongue out at him."

"That's not very ladylike."

Stu was speechless, just thinking how bloody beautiful she was, and finding it hard to take in the change before him.

"Living in a house full of men since me mum died, I'd nearly forgotten what it was like to doll myself up," Sandra said with a cheeky smile on her face.

"You look bloody fantastic." Stu blurted out a he moved towards her.

"Annie and I went shopping last weekend, and she took me round the boutiques in Brighton and 'voila', an instant Mod."

"Well your ride awaits outside."

"I hope it's cleaner on the inside than it is on the outside, I don't want to muck up my new gear."

"I cleaned it out personally." Stu joked

"So where are you taking me?"

"I want to show you off to my mates in the Pan Dor, make them jealous as hell.

"But that's a Mod hangout."

"Well you certainly look like a real Mod with that gear on."

Why Not Tonight- Mojos

If Sandra was nervous she didn't show it as they went up the narrow staircase to the Pam Dor which as usual was packed, smoke filled and noisy.

Bob, Col and Linda and a couple of others were at their usual table as Stu and Sandra pulled over a couple of chairs and joined them, and the conversation suddenly abated, all eyes on Sandra, obvious lust from the boys and a judged visual assessment by the girls.

It was Linda who spoke first, "Ain't you the bird from the beach in Brighton?"

"Yeah." Said Sandra, "The Rocker bird Stu pulled out of the sea and you helped me to his scooter to get to the hospital."

"But you look so different."

"I wasn't at me best that day." Laughed Sandra.

"But your clothes and fantastic shoes, they are totally Mod and fab."

"It's a miracle what a dab of makeup and some new gear can make, ain't it?

"But you were a Rocker." Linda stated.

"Well you have to move with the times, things change, people change, fashion changes and at the end of the day underneath we are all the same."

"I'll drink to that." Said Stu when somebody buys me a coffee."

"Hear you passed your driving test." Said Col, changing the subject.

"Yeah and brought meself a Morris minivan."

"You wanna sell your GS?" asked Bob hopefully.

"You have got to be joking, the love of my life."

A swift elbow in the ribs suddenly reminded him what he had said, "Sorry the other love in my life.", as he turned to Sandra and blew her a kiss.

"So, are you two together?" asked Sarah, one of the other girls on the table.

"Since Brighton we have seen each other a few times, Stu came to see if I was alright after the accident and it carried on from there."

"Yeah, I can understand that, he always had an eye for a pretty bird did our Stu, but a Rocker bird, that's a new one." Bob added.

"Maybe he saw something in me that appealed to him regardless of how I dressed or what I was." Sandra said, her voice taking on a raw edge.

"OK that's enough about us, so what have you lot being doing?" Stu asked trying to steer the conversation away from Sandra.

"Not a lot." Answered Col, "Buying a few records, got some new Tamla Motown originals which are really cool, got them in The Smoke when I was up there last time and have practically worn them out on my old Dansette record player."

"I can vouch for that." Linda said, "Just plays them over and over."

"A new group called the Kinks are playing at the pier on the third of July, five bob for an advanced ticket." Chirped in Bob

"I saw 'em up at Muswell Hill in North London, they ain't half bad, so maybe it might be worth going to see them." Col added.

Stu could sense that Sandra was beginning to feeling uncomfortable with her enforced surroundings and decided it was time to go, "Gonna give me minivan a bit of a spin to check her out so me and Sandra are off."

Pushing their way through the Pam Dor crowd Stu turned to Sandra and asked her "Where do you wanna go?"

"Let's go to the beach?"

"Bit late for a swim." Stu joked.

"No, go along to the beach behind the Cooden Beach Hotel." Sandra insisted.

"Thought that would be the last place you would want to go, right near where you work."

"When I have finished cleaning the rooms I often take my break and walk on the beach, I love the sound and the smell of the sea."

The road that ran alongside, the Cooden Beach Hotel at Little Common led to a quiet stretch of shingle beach away from the main road and although it was dark the moonlight gave it a surreal look reflecting off of the sea.

"I like it here, you can get away from all of your troubles here, it is so calm and peaceful." Sandra said as she looked out to sea.

"I am sorry if you felt uncomfortable back at the Pam Dor, they are not a bad crowd really and we have all been friends for a long time, and maybe it was stupid off me to drag you there."

"It would be the same if you came into the Rocker café with me, but your friends all gathered round to help me when I needed help, even when they found out I was a Rocker, so they can't be all that bad."

"It's been the fucking press that have created this fucking rift between the Mods and Rockers, before Clacton they never mentioned the subject, now every Bank Holiday they fill their front pages with ridiculous headlines of violence and roaming groups of warring youngsters."

Sandra leaning across and kissed Stu with a passion she had not felt before, her tongue exploring his mouth, her arms pulling him closer, his hand cupping her breast, her nipples hardening to his touch. Slowly she pushed his hand down across her stomach, her intention clear.

Stu pulled up her skirt running his hand up her stockings until he reached the bare skin above the stocking tops and then as she opened her legs he felt the wetness of her knickers.

"Is there room in the back of this passion wagon?" Sandra suggested seductively.

"Why do you think I brought a minivan?"

Sandra pulled the door cord and got out of the car and in one deft movement pulled her dress over her head, "Don't want to screw-up me new dress, do I?"

Opening the rear doors, standing just in her knickers, bra and suspender belt she peered inside and turned to Stu who was pulling off his jeans, "You could have put a bloody mattress in here."

"I've only just got the bloody thing and I surely didn't expect to be christening the back of the van tonight."

Sandra climbed in and turned to Stu who was fishing in his pocket for something. "What are you doing?"

"Looking for my Lucky Durex."

"Why Lucky?"

"Well I knew my luck must have changed to be using it." he laughed

Sandra watched as he tore the Durex out of the silver foil and pulling down his pants started to unroll the sheer rubber over his hardened prick.

Pulling her knickers down and exposing herself by opening her legs wide,

Stu crawled forward and lowered himself onto her his prick entering the warmth of her wet pussy as they clung to each other until they had both sated their desires.

"Next time a mattress," Sandra giggled, "or even better a real bed."

A Little Loving – Fourmost

"You look like the fucking cat that got the cream." Paul said as Stu turned up on his GS, the smile still spread across his face from the night before.
"Had a good night, that's all."
"Sandra?"
Stu nodded, as he climbed off his Vespa, and pulled it onto its stand.
"So, who were you last night, Stu the Mod, Stu the Rocker or Minivan Man?"
"Minivan Man."
"I don't know how you are getting away with it."
"Took Sandra down the Pam Dor."
"Jesus, you are really living on the edge."
"No, it was OK Sandra looked great as a Mod, looked just like Cathy McGowan, stunning."
"What did her brother say about that?"
"Jim was Ok about it, practically as shocked as me."
It was John Piddock coming out of his office that suddenly halted the conversation, and he had a face on him and that was never a good sign.
"We got a visitor coming down from London today, so keep busy and whatever he wants he gets. Understand?"
"Not that geezer in the Jaguar?" Paul asked.
"Yeah, Dave King, coming down for his regular two monthly visits and if he doesn't get treated right he can turn rough, if you know what I mean?"
"What has he got over you?" Stu asked.
"I borrowed money from his lot to keep the business running when I had hit some hard times and when the banks refused me and now the interest on the debt just keeps mounting up."
"Who are his lot?" Stu asked.
"You don't wanna know, the less you know about them the better."
"Fuck you make 'em sound like the Mafia." Paul ventured.
"This lot make the Mafia look like pussycats." John admitted.
"If there is anything we can do, just ask." Stu stated.

It was just after eleven that the Jag rolled onto the forecourt and pulled up by the pumps, "Fill her up." Demanded the driver, and Tim who worked the pumps promptly filled the Jaguar's fuel tanks.
"Is that cash or cheque?" Tim asked.
"Lose it sonny." Said the driver Dave King "And I want this motor cleaned, so fetch one of the grease monkeys from outback.
In the passenger seat sat a leggy blonde who just sat there polishing her nails, taking little interest in what was going on around her.
 Paul duly arrived took the keys, "Touch anything in that car and I'll break your fucking arms and legs. So, give it a wax and wash and get it back to me pronto."
"OK." Said Paul biting his lip and desperately trying to stop himself punching the arsehole in the face, but he knew that would be of no help to anybody.

"And your daughter, does she want to stay in the car or have a cup of coffee?" Paul asked guessing that the moll was hardly likely to be related to this short-arsed punk standing in front of him.

"She ain't my daughter, you lippy little shit, just get on with it."

Paul climbed into the car, turned on the engine and selected drive on the automatic gearbox and drove the car to the back of the garage and the workshops.

The young woman got out lit a cigarette and leant against the wall looking bored as Stu and Paul hosed down the car and dried it before starting to wax the car over.

"Jesus, that guy is a total cunt. Why the hell did John get involved with these fucking crooks?"

"By the sound he didn't have much choice, he was in desperate in need of cash to keep his garage going and these guys must have seemed like the solution to his problems."

"There must be something we can do to help."

John looked washed out when the Jag finally pulled away, his face drawn and pale.

"Bad?" Paul asked.

"About as bad as it gets, they have upped the repayments and he is coming back on the 1st of August for the next instalment."

"What you gonna do?"

"Pray for a heart attack or hope to win the Littlewood's Football Pools." Admitted John.

Later that evening Stu sat round the table with Sandra's dad and Jim and related the day's events.

"Is there nothing we can do to help John out?" Stu asked.

"I've known John for donkey's years and one thing he is not is a crook, these bastards have got him over a barrel. We have got a few weeks before this little punk comes back so we have to put our minds together and come up with something.

"John is really afraid of this guy and those he works for. They sound a pretty hard."

"They and scum like them who are involved with the London gangs are into every illegal operation under the sun, drugs, protection, prostitution, you name it and they got their sticky fingers in it."

"You seem to know a lot about them?"

"Part of my job."

"Your job?"

"Surely Sandra has told you I am a detective based over in Hastings."

"A copper?" Stu asked the shock evident in his response, "If John knew I was talking to the police he would never forgive me."

"This conversation never happened." Sandra's dad said tapping his nose.

"August 1st that's the next Bank Holiday Weekend." Said Sandra.

"Did you see this in the Bexhill Observer." Sandra asked pushing the paper in front of Stu.

"What?"

"The headlines here."

Stu looked at the paper, the only headline he could see was that a German mine had been found on the beach.

"So?"

"Look more carefully where they found it."

73

Stu quickly read the article and his face went pale.

"Fuck!"

"Well fuck indeed, the paper reckons that some irresponsible motorist drove onto the beach during the night exposing the mine just behind the Cooden Beach Hotel and when it was discovered the next day by a man walking his dog, the Bomb Disposal Team had to be called and the road closed and the nearby hotel evacuated.

"Was it where we were?

Sandra nodded, "I could hardly keep a straight face."

"That would have been a hell of a bang."

"Well I thought it was."

"You are terrible." Steve quipped hardly able to keep for laughing out loud.

Wishin' and Hopin'- Merseybeats

Ever since the fateful visit in June, Stu and Paul had been putting their heads together to see what they could do to help John in his predicament, and had persuaded everybody they knew to buy petrol at Winchelsea Road Garage which had helped, but not enough.

"There has got to be something." Stu declared.

"So, what have we got to go on, one: he will demand a fill up of fuel which he will not pay for, two: each visit he has demanded we clean his car, three: he leaves back tyre marks as he pulls out of the garage on his way back to London." Paul recounted using his fingers to make the points.

"Fill his car with diesel, which wouldn't be a first for Tim." Stu suggested with a smile.

"Too obvious, we at least need him to leave the garage but not get very far."

"How far do you think he would get I we drained the engine and transmission oil?"

"With the residue coating of oil inside the engine after we have drained it and if he guns the Jag away as usual maybe five to ten minutes. How can you be so sure?

"When I forgot to refill the oil in Mr Parfitt's A35, that didn't make it to the seafront before the pistons came through the bonnet." Sniggered Paul.

"What about loosening the prop shaft, just leave one bolt holding it on." Stu added.

Paul scratched his chin, and Stu could see his brain ticking over.

"If we put the car straight into the workshop over the inspection pit while one of us cleans it and the other does the dirty deed we might just have enough time."

"Ok how does that help John, that bastard will still have the money and will be away from here?"

"That's where we could do with a little help from our friends." Paul suggested.

"I have an idea." Said Stu.

It was late on Thursday evening when Stu on his GS and Col, Bob, Mick the Mod, Grey and a couple of others pulled up outside of the Bathing Pool in St Leonards only to find a line of Rockers on their motorbikes already there and even as they switched off their engines more Rockers arrived.

Like two medieval armies they lined up facing each other, handlebar to handlebar.

Directly in front of Stu sat Paul and Jim on the bikes and to his surprise Sandra sat there dressed from head to foot in leather on her Tiger Cub.

Dismounting Stu walked over to his friends as his fellow Mods looked on.

"Gather round." Stu turned and beckoned his friends forward, at the same time the Rockers dismounted.

You could feel the unease in the air, suspicion evident on their assembled faces as Paul continued.

"As I have explained and I expect Paul has done the same, our boss John Piddock has found himself in deep shit, with some fucking mobsters screwing him into the ground because of mounting debt and it is because of this we need your help. On Saturday the 1st August one particularly despicable arsehole is coming down from London to collect money from John, and this is where we need your help." Explained Stu.

Paul took up the discussion, "We need all of you to help us by causing a distraction, a fight."

A couple of the Rockers rubbed their hands gleefully, before Paul gave them a withering look.

"When he leaves the garage, I need the motorbikes to fall in around him, like an escort to until you reach the junction of Elphinstone Road opposite the Crematorium where the Mods will be assembled, and it is there we will strike." Stu and I reckon that after a number of small modifications to his Mk10 Jag it should be having some difficulties by the time it reaches the Crematorium on The Ridge and it is there we need you to block the road with your scooters in case the Jag gets that far. We need to get him out of the car while either Stu or I can get into the car and retrieve John's money.

"If all goes well we can get John his money back without this arsehole making any sort of connection to him and what is going on around him." Stu added.

"How will he know this ain't a put-up job?" Demanded one of the Rockers.

"With all the crap the newspapers have made about the Mods and Rockers fighting each other I can't see that he could suspect a pre-organised plan."

"Do we have an agreement?" Demanded Paul, as he scanned the faces around him, noting the nods of approval.

Slowly the group dispersed as Stu walked over to Sandra who was still astride her motorcycle, "What are you doing here?" he demanded.

"Didn't want to miss the fun did I." she said with a mischievous grin on her face.

Leaning forward Stu kissed her, and whispered "You look really good in those leathers."

"I could look even better out of them." She giggled.

When everyone had left except Stu and Sandra a figure appeared out of the shadows and approached the couple.

"I want a word with you." Demanded the intruder.

Stu turned to be confronted by Sandra's father, "Have you been there all the time?

"Long enough, but I want you to give John Piddook my direct telephone number and to call me as soon as this King fellow drives away from garage, that is if he leaves without paying for the fuel. There is nothing I can do about the extorsion but if he leaves the garage without paying for the fuel he would have committed a crime and I can get him on that."

"But what about the rest of what you heard?" Stu asked.

"The rest of what?" he asked with a sly wink before he turned and left.

"Why didn't you tell me before that your old man was a copper?

"Thought it might put you off me and I didn't want that to happen. Most blokes run a mile when they found out me dad was a copper."

"Now what was you saying about getting out of your leathers?"

"Me dads at work tonight and Jim is out with his mates and my little bed is empty…….."

It's All Over Now-The Rolling Stones

"Ten bob for a ticket to see the Stones on Saturday." Moaned Linda.

"What do you expect they are Number One in the charts this week." Col reminded her. You going Stu?"

"Yeah got tickets for me and Sandra and looking forward to it, that is if everything goes to plan Saturday morning.

"You reckon it is still going ahead?" asked Bob.

"John had a phone call that they were expecting his payment in full or if not, he could be experiencing a visit to the local hospital for treatment."

"Bastards." Col muttered more to himself.

"What about the Rockers, can they be trusted?"

"Jim and Paul have got everything in hand on their side, I have no doubt they will play their part."

"Well I hope they are not too enthusiastic when it comes to the 'fight', I know it has got to look realistic but not too realistic if you know what I mean."

It was Mick the Mod pushing his way towards them through the Friday evening crowd in the Pam Dor, a grave look on his face."

"What's up?" Stu asked

"You ain't gonna believe this but I was working up in Battersea on a plastering job for my gaffer all the local Mods were all talking about next weekend and how they were gonna enjoy coming to Hastings for a bit of aggro or as they put it, for The Second Battle of Hastings."

"Suppose it had to happen, done Clacton, Margate and Brighton, Hastings seems the next logical choice."

"Why couldn't they have done Southend for a change?" Stu said, trying to work out how much this new information could fuck-up their plans, "Could be loads more coppers about which could screw everything up. I need to go and see Paul to see what he has heard."

Paul's Bonneville was chained up in his front garden, which was a relief to Stu as he rarely went anywhere without it. Walking up the front steps he rapped on the front door.

"Am I pleased you were in." Stu said as the door opened, "Just heard some worrying news, it seems Hastings is the target for next weekend's invasion."

"Yeah I heard the rumour and Jim's dad had some intelligence reports confirming it.

"You've seen Jim?"

"Just got back."

"Do you think it will make any difference to our plan?"

"Should be early enough in the day before most Mods and Rockers arrive, excepting those who have come down to see the Stones. Gonna have to play it by ear."

"We gotta make it work to help John, and if he loses the garage we lose our jobs. It's more than just his money riding on this."

"I don't want you anywhere near when we catch up the King on Saturday." Stu said seriously, as Sandra stood before him.

"If you and Jim are there I can't stay at home worrying about you both."

"You must promise me that you will not get involved." Stu pleaded.

"I can look after myself." Sandra stated defiantly.

"Well keep right out of the way, I just don't know how this is going to play out."

"I think you need a distraction." As she ran her hand up his thigh and rested it where she knew it would have an effect.

Stu felt his penis hardening under her gentle caresses and he turned to kiss her she leaned forward undoing his fly and finding the object she was searching for and freeing it from his underpants gently kissed it before closing her mouth around it and using her tongue on it.

Stu just sank back into his seat as Sandra worked her magic.

"Are you alright down there?" he whispered.

Halting her rhythmic action on his prick, she looked up with an impish smile on her face, "My dad said not to talk with my mouth full."

It didn't take long before he could hold himself any longer and he came with her mouth still around his prick.

"Christ where did you learn to do that?"

"You would be surprised at what we see in the hotel, and for that matter what we find when the guests have left, dirty books amongst other things."

"I never thought of the Cooden Beach Hotel had that kind of clientele."

"You would be surprised at what some of the golf widows get up to while their hubbies hit a silly ball around the golf course."

"Now." she said, "It is my turn." Turning to Stu as she pulled up her skirt and wriggled out of her knickers, and kicking them into the footwell of the mini, opening her legs and leaving her wanting pussy exposed.

Stu found her wetness and gently pushed his finger into her, and gently rubbed her clitoris as she groaned quietly, before she put her hands on his head and drew his face down onto her where he continued with his tongue until she cried out in pleasure until she felt the ripples of an orgasm.

I Get Around- The Beach Boys

As the week progressed John Piddock had grown more reclusive hardly leaving his office while Stu and Paul continued working through the customer's cars that continued to arrive for their repairs and servicing. It was obvious that he was not coping well with the pressure on his life.

For Paul and Stu everything was in place. Col would be waiting at the junction of Elphinstone Road opposite the Crematorium on The Ridge and Jim would be waiting in Rock Lane for the Jaguar to leave the garage which was in plain sight of their position. Paul kept looking at his watch as the minutes ticked by waiting for the Jaguar to arrive.

"Do you think he is coming?" Stu asked nervously.

"I fucking hope so." Paul answered,

In preparation the inspection pit was clear of cars and was ready to drive the Jaguar straight in and over it.

"That's it, he is here." Shouted Stu as he saw the Jaguar pull up at the pumps.

Stu watched Tim walk over to the car and although he could not hear the conversation he could see he had gone to the fuel filler cap and had undone it before putting in the nozzle to deliver the petrol.

Paul walked up to John's office and watched as Tim finished filling the car before he walked onto the forecourt.

"You." Demanded Dave King as he noticed Paul, "Get this car fucking cleaned and I want to see my reflection in the paintwork. Understand?"

Paul nodded and took the car keys from the King, before jumping in the car. Beside him the young woman looked bored and continued to look out of the side window.

As he reached the workshop doors he stopped the car for the young woman to get out as he drove across to the inspection pit where Stu stood guiding him forward before jumping down into the pit ready to drain the sump and gearbox. Within seconds the hot oil was pouring into the drain tin on the floor, while he set to with his spanner on the retaining bolts of the drive shaft.

Above him Paul worked furiously with sponge and soapy water to clean the car and dry it before waxing it.

In the doorway the young woman watched nonchalantly smoking a cigarette. To Stu's eyes she did not in fact look much older than himself, her tight skirt and rib hugging jumper doing nothing to disguise her well-proportioned body only spoilt by heavy makeup that gave the impression of a tart.

"With his job done Stu joined Paul as they dried off the car before applying the wax and polishing the paint work to a mirror-like finish.

"You done?" demanded John from his office door while King stood behind him looking bloody pleased with himself.

"Just about." Replied Paul, as he finished buffing up the chrome.

"Then bring it around front."

Even as he reversed it out of the garage the rumble of the loose prop shaft was audible to his trained ear but hopefully not to the gorilla out front.

The young woman got into the car taking a long look at Paul but not saying anything as he drove the Jag onto the forecourt, deliberately gunning the engine a few times.

Even before Paul had exited the car King was hustling him out of the way to continue his journey.

As the Jag pulled away he turned to Tim, "Did he pay for the petrol?"
Tim shook his head.
"Good."
The sound of the motorbikes caused Paul to turn as he watched the bikes taking up position behind the Jag.
"So far so good." He muttered to himself, as he rushed to jump on his motorbike and to join them.

Stu looked down at John slumped his chair, broken and dejected.
"You gotta ring the police."
"What can they do? I am in this shit because of my own fucking fault."
Stu picked up the phone and reading the number on the piece of paper dialled the number Sandra's dad had given him.
"Detective Inspector David Phillips." Came the response.
"It's Stu, our friend has left without paying for his petrol, reckon if you get up to the Crematorium in the next five minutes or so you might find him."
Stu replaced the receiver and turned to John, "I need to go out for a few minutes."

In the Jaguar the prop shaft was becoming increasingly noisy and the engine was running rather rough and just to add to King's problems the car was now surrounded by motorbikes, some in front slowing him down with Rockers grinning and gesturing all around him, while the rest followed.
"Fucking punks." He shouted through the open driver's window only to be followed by more abuse.
With the car running more erratically, the blonde turned to him and said, "Maybe we are running out of petrol?"
King turned in his seat his face like thunder, "We have just filled the fucking car with petrol, you stupid cunt."
The blonde turned her head and she looked out across the town of Hastings and the sea beyond, a smile on her face.
It had not taken Paul long to catch up with the little convoy and as he arrived the car suddenly ground to a halt, steam and smoke belching from the engine compartment, and they were only a couple of hundred yards from the Crematorium gates.
The Mods on their scooters now streamed down the road to join the confusion surrounding the stricken car, hurling abuse at the Rockers and waving their fists in the air, and soon the road was totally blocked with youngsters in some kind of victory celebration, completely confusing him.
The arrival of a police car and Black Maria brought momentary relief to King as the police moved through the throng of hooligans, separating them.
"What seems to be the problem here? The plain clothes detective asked.
"My car had broken down and these fucking Mods and Rockers are having their own private war." King explained as he got out of the car.
Checking the car's number plate, Detective Inspector Phillips, looked directly at King, "I have received information this vehicle driven by yourself have just stolen ten pounds worth of petrol from a filling station in Ore Village."
"What the fuck are you talking about? What stolen petrol.?"
"Have you just filled your car with petrol?"
"Well……"

"And of course, you have the receipt?" the detective inspector added.

"It's a mistake, I must have forgotten to pay because I was in a hurry to get back to London." King tied to explain as he suddenly spotted Paul in the crowd surrounding the car, "Ask that punk over there, he knows me and that it was a genuine misunderstanding."

"Dunno what you are talking about, just out for a ride on me Bonnie."

"I'm arresting you on suspicion of the theft of twenty gallons of petrol to the value of ten pounds from Winchelsea Road Garage and anything you say can be taken down in evidence......"

Paul walked over to the car and opened the passenger door, "It looks like you will be catching the train home darling as your boyfriend won't be driving this car any further as he has been arrested."

The young woman looked at Paul, "He ain't my boyfriend and I didn't think it would get this far after you drained the oil and it sounds like you had a go at the prop shaft as well."

"You saw us doing that and didn't say anything?" Paul asked the shock of their antics suddenly being exposed worrying him as he watched King being put into the back of the Black Maria.

"He was a bastard and deserves all he gets, a fucking bully."

"You seem to know a lot about cars?"

"My dad had a garage before these bastards put him out of business, I spent my life around cars and motorbikes before I was forced to be 'looked after' as a guarantee that my dad kept his gob shut."

"Like a hostage?"

"Something like that." She said quietly.

My name is Paul, sorry I don't know yours."

"Mandy, and by the way you ought to look down there behind the driver's seat for that bastard's cash box, he's been collecting all morning so there should be quite a stash in it, plus some more cash in the glove box."

"You didn't have to tell me about that."

"Nothing to do with me, give it to your boss to keep his garage going."

From the corner of his eye he saw Sandra and beckoned her over, "This is Mandy and she might need a lift somewhere or...." Paul hesitated, "or she might want to a stay down here for the weekend and I'll take her home."

"Haven't had a holiday by the seaside for years and I accept your kind offer of a lift home." Mandy said as she looked Paul directly in the eye.

By the time Stu arrived the excitement was over and around him Mods and Rockers stood talking to each other reminding him of a scene he had seen from the First World War where Germans and English soldiers had had a Christmas Truce in 1914 and mixed with each other in No-Mans-Land between the trenches.

"Come on Stu," Paul called as he mounted his Bonnie, "We gotta get back to John and explain what has happened."

John looked amazement when he opened the cash box, "There must be over two thousand quid in here. Where the hell did you get it?"

"Found it in the back of an old Jag, can you believe that?

"Not......"

"Yeah, Dave King's motor, must have run out of oil or something."

81

"Run out of oil?"

"You didn't have anything to do with that did you?" John asked Paul.

"Not me boss", looking towards Stu who stood with a broad grin on his face.

"Because it wouldn't be the first time you forgot to put oil in car would it?"

"Is there enough cash in there to pay off your debt?"

"And more." John said, looking at his watch, "You still have got fifteen minutes before we close, so tidy up and bugger off. I owe you two hooligans so keep out of trouble this weekend. You hear me?"

On The Beach-Cliff Richard

It was late afternoon when the group assembled down near the fishing huts on the beach in the Old Town, Col, Bob, Mick the Mod and Sandra who had reverted to her Mod dress after returning home and changing for Stu to pick her up on his GS.
"Worked like a fucking dream." Stu explained, John got his money back and enough to keep the garage going, that bastard Dave King got banged up by the police and I think Paul has fallen for this bird from London after Sandra here took her back to Paul's flat to wait for him,"
"When I left them, they were chatting about cars and from what I could see he could not keep his eyes off of her." Sandra explained.
"He deserves to find a good bird even though he is a Rocker." Stu said giving Sandra a sideways glance and a wink.
In the dense mass of Parka's, Col suddenly turned and greeted a Mod that Stu thought he recognised from last summer."
"Ain't that the Southend geezer, Steve who shagged Sarah last year?" Bob questioned.
"That's where I have seen him before," Stu replied as he noticed the girl standing beside Steve.
"Looks like he has brought his own talent with him this time." Bob said as he eyed-up the good-looking bird with more than a pang of jealousy.
"She looks a bit up market for you." Stu added, noticing his friend's lustful interest in the young woman,
"Her gear must have cost a fortune, looks like real designer stuff." Added Sandra joining into the conversation, noticing more than just her figure.
"What do yer mean, to up-market?" Bob protested.
"That bird has class." Sandra concluded.

Most of the rest of the afternoon the two rival factions were kept apart by a strong police presence, as Mods rode their scooters around the town and the Rockers did much the same on their bikes.
Stu was sure he saw Paul with that London bird on the back of his Bonnie with her wearing one of his old leather jackets and he was pleased for his friend and workmate who hadn't had a girlfriend for ages, mainly because his bike was the main thing in his life and birds did not like coming second to a machine.
"That was Paul on his Bonnie wasn't it and that girl?"
"Her name is Mandy and she is really nice, I had a long chat with her this morning when I took her back to Paul's flat, after the police took that bastard away. That bastard King used and abused her and she was happy as Larry when they carted him off."
"I'm gonna have get ready to see the Stones tonight, I need to freshen up after getting all hot and sweaty."
 "When did you get hot and sweaty it ain't that hot?"
"I haven't yet but we need to go back to my place to change and you know what that means, an empty house and just you and me."

The queue for the Stones show was getting longer by the minute but Stu and Sandra had got there early enough to be near the front with a bunch of other Hating's Mods and as they stood there smoking and laughing there was a tangible sense of excitement.

"Shame the Beatles have knocked the Stones off the number one position on the charts." Declared Mick the Mod.

"All the little girls prefer the Beatles, last time I saw them the smell of urine as they pissed themselves with excitement was overbearing." Bob said.

"The Stones ain't really a Mod band but they ain't bad." Mick added as he spotted Col and Linda, plus Steve and his posh looking bird as they walked up the queue.

"Here Col." Came the call from Mick the Mod, "Come and join us."

Even as they pushed into the line it was obvious that their intrusion was seriously pissing off those behind, "You fucking can't just push in, we've been queuing for ages. Get the fuck out of it."

Mick the Mod turned and walked back towards the most vocal protester, the look on his face and his balled fists should have warned him that his intentions were far from friendly.

"You got a problem arsehole?"

"This is a fucking queue, you just can't let these people push in."

"These are my friends, and I was saving a place for them. Understand?

Or is there something in that statement you have difficulty in understanding?"

Realising that any further discussion was going to end up in violence the mouthy Mod took the line of least resistance and shut up.

Turning to others in the queue Mick simply asked, "Anyone else got a problem with me mates joining me?"

The shuffling of feet and downward eyes seemed to indicate that nobody else was willing to take up the challenge.

Steve and his girlfriend moved in to the line next to Stu and Sandra as he looked back at the mouthy Mod behind, "I work with that arsehole back in Essex, thinks he is the dog's bollocks a real Ace Face."

"Well if he is wise he won't piss off Mick the Mod."

"This is Nika, she's Russian." Said Steve introducing his girlfriend.

"And this is Sandra, and I think I met you last year at some party down here or at the Pam Dor."

"Yeah I remember the party." Steve said with a smile, "My grandparents live just up in Hawkhurst and I was down here for my summer hols."

"And now you are back again."

"Yeah and by the look of it most the Mods in the south."

"Watch out there, there's an ambulance driving up here."

Sandra turned and caught a glimpse of the ambulance driver who much to her surprise was her father and she had to smile.

"That's how they are getting the Stones onto the pier." She said quietly to Stu, that's the old ambulance the police use I know I have seen it in the police compound."

"How do you know that?"

"Me dad was driving it." She smirked.

The music was pulsating and the Stones really got the audience behind them and when they played 'It's all over now' the crowd went wild.

Even Stu although not really the greatest Stones fan on the planet was caught up in the excitement and having seen the Stones in Hastings at least twice, this time they really had their shit together.

"God knows what my dad thought of the Stones when he drove them in." Sandra shouted above the music.

"Do you think he got their autographs?"

Sandra laughed out loud, shaking her head, "Not really his scene."

The Stones performance was all over too quickly, the supporting groups had been great and the atmosphere was still electric as the crowd came out into the cool evening air.

"You have had quite a day." Sandra whispered in his ear.

"One I won't forget in a while that's for sure, especially when we got back to your place."

"That's not what I meant." Sandra said as she wagged her finger in his direction, "But I know what you mean.".

"At least it feels like we helped John and he has been a good boss to work for and has taught me a hell of a lot, so I am pleased as the whole situation was really getting him down."

"Do you think it is all going to kick off tomorrow?" Sandra asked changing the subject.

"A lot of what you read in the papers is exaggerated, I know my old man believed the headlines plastered across the front pages of the Sun and the Mirror. 'Wild Ones Beat Up Seaside', and all that crap. Hell, I was there and it wasn't that violent. Of course, there some fights but no more than at most football matches on a Saturday night. There are always going to be some Mods or Rockers who want to fight,"

As they got back to where Stu parked his GS on the promenade Sandra looked out to sea, her eyes had that faraway look, I'm glad I cut my foot in Brighton, if I hadn't I would never have met you."

"And you might have met a nice Rocker boy and lived happily ever after."

"Bollocks." She said with a broad smile across her face in the moonlight, "I seem to have found the perfect compromise."

"Come on Rocker girl get on the back of me scooter so I can take you home."

I Found Out The Hard way- Four Pennies.

"It looks like a fucking garage here, scooters, motorbikes and now that fucking Mini parked in the drive." Stu's old man remonstrated, "You are gonna have to get rid of something."
"But I drive and use them all."
"Then you have more fucking money than sense, most normal people would be satisfied just with one means of transport."
"I ain't normal people." Stu shouted.
"No, you can say that again."

It was the AJS that Stu decided to ride today, get out of town and the trouble brewing there and get out into the country to enjoy the good weather. Donning his leather jacket and Bone Dome he set off for Bexhill to pick up Sandra, along the Bexhill Road that was already busy with Bank Holiday traffic including a large number of scooters heading in the opposite direction towards the seafront.
Sandra opened her front door and looked at Stu in his leathers than down at herself in a skirt, "Didn't know we were Rocker today so I had better go and change, Jim is through in the kitchen, go and grab a coffee and I'll be down in a tick."
"Want a coffee?" Jim asked as Stu made his way into the kitchen and sat down, "Her' just a tick' maybe some time." He added.
"Thought I'd take the bike for a spin today, make the most of the good weather."
"Saw Paul last night down the club, chuffed as hell with that bird from London, they sat and chatted about carburettors which for him was the equivalent of talking dirty. Apparently, she knows her way around engines because her old man had a garage and let her tinker with the cars, sounds to me like a match made in heaven."
"Thanks for everything yesterday, It worked out well."
"Good bit of fun and my old man made a good collar as that piece of shit was wanted for a number counts and is likely to be put away for some time."
"It took a load of pressure off of John."
"Looks like it all turned out alright."
Sandra reappeared clad from head to foot in her leather gear and waved a a photo in front of Stu's face, "Look what me dad got last night."
Stu took the photo and looked at the signatures, Mick Jagger, Keith Richards, Brian Jones, Bill Wyman and Charley Watts.
"And he asked them to make it out to me." Sandra said, "Look 'To Sandra' it says."
"I don't expect they were gonna argue with a detective inspector."
"So, where we going?" Sandra demanded.
"Thought we could ride out to Bodiam Castle. Get away from the town for a few hours"
"Sounds like a plan to me, so come on let's go."

Leaving the bike in the car park Stu and Sandra walked hand in hand across the grass towards the castle enjoying just being together away from Hastings and the social complications of their friendship, here they could just be themselves."
"I wish Jim could find a nice girl friend, especially now Paul has found someone."
"I am sure when the right bird comes along he will know."
Stu sank down onto the grass pulling Sandra down next to him and they both lay down and looked up into the blue sky, drinking in the quietness of their surroundings.

It was the sudden shadows that fell across them that alerted Stu that they were not alone and he sat up.

"Well look here a fucking Rocker and his tart spoiling our view."

Stu stood up slowly and pulling Sandra to her feet and looked at the three Mod couples that stood leering at them, looking confident and threatening.

For Stu this was a new experience, seeing the world from the other side of the fence as a Rocker. Studying the Mods in front of him Stu recognised the type.

"They look like they come from South London, Streatham probably," Stu observed out loud, "You can tell that by the shit quality of their suits, they are what Mods call 'tickets', bad Mods, someone still wearing last week's fashion, slightly grown-out hair, and not enough or too many mirrors on their scooters."

"A ticket?" Sandra asked as innocently as she could.

"Yeah like the railway ticket," Stu paused and turned and faced the Mods, "Definitely third class."

"That's it, you lippy cunt, now you're gonna get it."

Even as he had finished speaking Sandra had leapt forward like a wild cat attacking her prey, kicked him between the legs and as he fell forward karate chopped him across the neck and he went down like a sack of potatoes.

Stu headbutted the second Mod as he stood mouth wide open at Sandra's surprise attack on his mate. "You've broken my fucking nose you fucking arsehole." He screamed clutching his face trying to staunch the flow of blood. Stu then drove his fist into his unprotected stomach forcing him to drop to his knees, winded and out of the fight.

"Two down one to go." Shouted Stu as he watched the two Mods writhing on the ground

Sandra now turned on the three Mod girls who were backing away from this wild Rocker girl, "Come three of you against little old me, that's fair odds."

The third male Mod just stood there transfixed to the spot unable to do anything as Stu approached him, "Don't hit me."

"What's the matter don't wanna get blood on your suit?" Stu taunted him.

"Just leave me alone." The Mod. cringed waiting for the punch to arrive.

"You're not even worth the effort. Now when your little friends have recovered get on your fucking scooters and piss off home and pray you don't meet any real rockers because they will eat you for breakfast."

"You OK?" Stu called to Sandra who was still circling the three Mod girls.

"This one has pissed herself and I haven't even hit her yet."

"Leave them alone, they have learnt their lesson and seen these losers for what they are, full of shit beaten by one fucking Rocker and his tart."

Stu and Sandra turned away and started to walk back to the car park.

"Where did you learn those moves?" Stu asked,"

"Me dad taught me to defend myself, just in case I ever gone in a difficult spot."

"Remind me never to piss you off."

Do Wah Diddy Diddy- Manfred Mann

Stu pulled into a line of motorbikes on the way back to Hastings, but turned off at The Ridge to go back to Bexhill via Catsfield, a route he thought would be less fraught with trouble, He had had enough excitement for one day and had learnt not to piss off Sandra after seeing her action.

"What do you wanna do tonight?" Sandra asked as they arrived back at her place.

"I dunno."

"Well at least come in for a coffee."

"OK."

Sandra's dad was home as they came in through the front door and the smell coming from the kitchen reminded Stu that he hadn't eaten much during the course of the day.

"Hope you two have had a nice afternoon," David Phillips inquired as they entered the kitchen.

"Went out to Bodiam Castle for a ride."

"Probably the best place to have gone, the town was heaving with holiday makers and Mods and Rockers, stretching the police force to their limits."

"Stu was impressed you got the Rolling Stones autographs."

"Got roped in to driving them to and from the Pier after their performance, nice boys not what I expected."

"Sandra said that she had thought that she had seen you driving the old ambulance down the pier."

"They couldn't spare anybody else to do." David Phillips admitted.

"OK let's eat."

For Stu the idea of eating with a detective inspector would have seemed totally alien to him a few weeks ago, but through Sandra he had seen a different side of her father, the copper, and how his own life had become entwined with Jim being the best friend of his workmate and now the incident with Dave King and all that involved, not to mention his double life as a Mod and Rocker and finally how he felt for Sandra.

As Sandra washed up after the meal her father took Stu into the front room and Stu could see he wanted to say something to him.

"Was there anything else in that car that I should have known about?"

Stu hesitated not knowing whether to tell the truth or act in ignorance. Deciding to tell him the truth he started, "There was a cash box which contained a large sum of money in it and some cash in the glove compartment which we gave to John Piddock to compensate him for his involvement with those bastards."

"Good." Said David Phillips, "He told us that he was just forgetful when he left the garage, but we were all too aware of what he was really doing down here, collecting protection money and debts, and of course we have no way of proving that even if we had the cash box as we have no idea of where else he had been collecting. What might interest you to know that even if he gets off with a light custodial sentence for petrol theft that is nothing to what the gang will do to him when he has to admit he hasn't got the money and he had lost it. I can't see them believing the story about the Mods and Rockers involvement in his arrest. So, all in all and good result all round, and of course I know nothing about what you handed to John and I don't want to know. John

Piddock has been a friend for many years and I know he is an honest man all I need him to do is confirm the theft of the petrol when I interview him about the crime."

"What about the young woman who was in the car with King?" Stu asked.

"What young woman?" David Phillips answered, with a look of total innocence, "No one has suggested there was any young woman involved."

"What are you two chatting about?" Sandra demanded when she had finished washing up.

"Nothing much just talking about cars." Stu answered.

"Right I'm on duty tonight so I have got to get back to the station for my shift, all hands to the deck as we are seriously shorthanded but that should all change tomorrow." David Phillips declared with a hint of resignation in his voice.

With the closing of the front door behind her father as he left for work, Sandra gave Stu one of her looks, "Got a feeling I am going to get hot and sweaty again."

Hold Me- P J Proby

With the GS polished and ready to go, Stu donned his Parka, and was ready to enjoy this Bank Holiday Monday, the weather remained fine and he felt comfortable back in his Mod gear. He still had a smile on his face from last night and you never knew what the new day would bring.

As he rode along the seafront he felt sorry for all the Mods who had been forced to sleep on the beach, but that was all part of these weekends and this time he had been at home and slept in his own bed.

As he passed Col's parent's house in Undercliff Terrace he could see a row of scooters parked outside, with a couple he did not recognise, but probably belonged to his mates from Southend he assumed.

Traffic was already building up along the Bexhill Road as he gunned the 160cc Vespa feeling the wind on his face, not the same as being on the AJS but still exhilarating in a different way.

This was the last Bank Holiday before Christmas and he was determined to make the most of it.

By the time he reached Sandra's place he was feeling well chuffed with himself and was looking forward to the forthcoming day.

"So, where are we going today?" Sandra asked as she opened the door.

"Thought we could go down the Old Town and catch up with the crowd, see what we missed yesterday?"

"Sounds good."

"I expect they are wondering where I got to."

"Probably best not to tell everything." Sandra smiled as she grabbed her jacket.

The town was packed and finally after finding a place to park the scooter by the cricket ground Stu and Sandra set off towards the Old Town and the fishing net huts which was where they usually met up.

The seafront was packed with Mods everywhere enjoying the sunshine, eating 99's or bags of chips as Stu looked for his friends. There were so many bodies around it made searching difficult, but Stu soon spotted Mick the Mod who stood head and shoulders above a huddle of Mods over in the coach park.

"Hey Mick how's it hanging?"

"Not bad, just listening to them Mods over there talking to the reporter about a frenzied Rocker attack on them yesterday, sounded fucking hairy."

Stu turned to look over at the group and was well surprised to see the Mods they encountered yesterday at Bodiam Castle, so he moved to within hearing distance.

"They came at us like fucking animals, them stinking greasers."

"How many of them were there?" the reporter asked.

"At least half a dozen, armed with chains and knives."

"And you managed to escape?"

"Not before we did for a couple of them." The Mod boasted."

"Is this normal?"

"Yeah, they hunt in packs like wild fucking animals, that's why when we see the greasers on the beach we get them before they get us."

"Is that where you got hurt?" Said the reported pointing at the plaster across the boy's nose.

Stu fed up with hearing this crap pushed his way through the small crowd and stood before the Mod who was still intent on talking to the reporter.

"And I suppose it was you who thrashed these fucking Rockers?" shouted Stu.

"Yeah, fucking gave one of them a good beating." The Mod boasted turning to look at Stu and the realisation struck him that here before him was the bloke that had nutted him, "That's one of them fucking Rockers." He shouted pointing at Stu.

The crowd turned and looked at Stu standing there in his Parka.

"Well he don't look like a fucking Rocker to me." Mick the Mod announced in a voice that all could clearly hear, "And in any case, this is my friend who I know is a Mod."

"But……" The boy started to say but got lost for words, turning to his two friends for support.

Stu smiled and added, "You know what these London Mods are like probably attacked a couple of old grannies who turned around and beat the shit out of them."

"No, it was Rockers," He protested.

"Outnumbered where you?" demanded Stu, "Then you are lucky to still be in one piece." Looking at the Mod's two friends who were studying the ground in front of them Stu nodded in their direction and these are the other brave Mods who did for the Rockers are they?

"I tell you this prick and his girlfriend over there are Rockers."

Mick the Mod moved towards the boy, drawing himself up to his full height before looking down on him, "I think you may have popped a few too many of your little purple pills and you are seeing things, We, are all fucking Mods here you stupid arsehole, so stop feeding this reporter a line of shit about your bravery and fuck off."

The Mod backed away joined by his two friends and their girlfriends and edged away ensuring they stayed a safe distance from Stu who just stood there and smiled.

As the girls passed Sandra, she leant forward, "Is that fear I smell, no I'm wrong it smells like piss, I though you may have changed your knickers by now."

Wide eyed with fear the girl shuffled past hardly daring to look back, remembering the look she saw in the Rocker girls eyes the day before.

"Jesus what is the world coming to when those little pricks can't tell a Mod from a Rocker, sorta worrying ain't it."

"So where is Col and the others?" Stu inquired.

"Ain't seen them today yet."

"Didn't get into any aggro yesterday did you?"

"No, mostly just rode around the town on our scooters and ended up at a party up in Upper Park Road."

"Think that friend of his from Southend and his bird stayed over with him last night."

"Better go and see if they are OK." Stu said as he put his arm around Sandra and heading back to where he had left his GS.

"Don't think they expected to see you today, those tickets. Poor sod couldn't believe his eyes when you stepped up to him, thought he was gonna puke." Said Sandra.

As they reached the scooter they realised they had company, the three Mod couples had followed them and Stu was sure it wasn't to thank them.

Stu turned, "I thought you might have learned your lesson yesterday."

"So, it was you and this fucking little tart." Bandage Nose shouted, as he balled his fists and moved forward, "This time I am ready for you."

"Well what's going on here?" came a voice from behind as two Rockers appeared.

Now Bandage Nose was confused, as were his two friends, who looked at Stu then back at the two advancing Rockers.

"Hi sis, these little shits giving you any trouble?" Shouted Jim.

"They had a go at us yesterday at Bodiam, and we gave them a bit of a beating but apparently they didn't get the message, even after I kicked one in the balls."

"I did warn them that if they met any real Rockers the could be in for some real trouble." Said Stu.

Paul had an evil grin on his face as he cracked his knuckles in anticipation and turned to Jim, "These must be the hard Mods we hear about."

"I don't fucking understand this fucked up place, it don't make sense." Shouted Bandage Nose as the two Rockers walked towards him.

"Go on Stu, take Sandra, we can deal with these arseholes." Called Paul.

Sandra walked over to the three Mod girls cowering against the wall, "As much as I would like to beat the shit out of you for not taking my advice, I really think you should start thinking about taking the train home because I suspect that your boyfriends may be visiting casualty before the day is out."

By the time Stu had engaged first gear and started to accelerate away, Paul and Jim were having a bit of fun slapping the little shitheads about, their cries echoing up the road.

That Girl Belongs To Yesterday- Gene Pitney

Stu was surprised at all the scooters parked outside of Col's parents place in Undercliff Terrace. It looked like everybody had turned up there.

Finding a parking space behind the Marina Building, Stu and Sandra pushed the front door open to find everybody deep in discussion, hardly noticing their arrival.

Finding Linda by the door to the living room gave Stu the chance to ask what was going on.

"You know that bird with Steve, the Russian one, Nika, well it turns out she is some Russian diplomat's daughter who had gone missing and is now the centre of a massive search." Explained Linda.

"How the hell did he come to be with her?"

"Picked her up in Hawkhurst near some secret Russian safe house, can you believe that?"

"Steve has worked out a plan to get her out of Hastings under the very noses of the police who are here in great numbers including some that flew into Lydd Airport as reinforcements. They are putting blocks on the roads and rounding up Mods and marching them out of town in an effort to spot her."

"So, how is this plan gonna work?" Stu asked.

"He has made some sort of arrangement with the Rockers down at the Bathing Pool, and we are all heading off there now."

"An arrangement with the Rockers?" Stu asked more out of interest than surprise"

"He knows one of the Southend Rockers who came down here, a friend of his from way back and he has agreed to help."

"This I must see." Said Sandra.

The whole group of Mods set off on their scooters along the promenade towards the Bathing Pool area, with Steve in the lead with the Russian bird on the pillion.

It seemed like déjà vu to Stu who like Steve had met up with the Rockers here just a day or so ago in a similar plan to join forces.

Stu and Sandra watched as Steve donned leathers and the Russian bird slipped on a leather jacket and helmet making her look like any other Rocker bird and mounted the motorbike, while his friend, the Rocker put on a Parka as was joined by a Mod girl he did not know but looked similar in stature and hair colour to the Russian girl and mounted Steve's Vespa Sportique.

Col called Stu over to outline the plan," Steve and the girl are riding the motorbike and are heading off to Hailsham hoping that the police will not be looking for the girl on a motorbike while his friend Fred and Razzle one of the Mod girls from Essex are going to ride through Bexhill as a decoy."

"What can we do?"

"Follow the scooter to give them a bit of support and once through Little Common take them across country to Hailsham."

Stu watched the Mod Steve take off on the BSA Gold Star and knew exactly what Steve must be feeling with all that power between his legs, and followed by a group of Rockers on motorbikes, Stu set off behind the Rocker turned Mod on the red Vespa Sportique, along the De La Warr Road, then on through Bexhill towards Little Common.

It was Stu who noticed the police at the roundabout at Little Common stopping scooters and questioning their riders and passengers, especially if they were female. The policeman stood in the road with his had indicating the scooters stop, and indicated they pull into the kerb.

"Where are you heading?" The policeman asked.

"We are all off to Brighton." Sandra shouted, "Why are you stopping us we ain't done nothing wrong."

"We are looking for a Russian girl with dark hair believed to be travelling on a scooter."

"Well we ain't Russian and my friend on the other scooter is from Essex, so you are wasting your time."

"Can't your friend speak for herself."

"Do I look or sound like a fucking Russian." Razzle said in a hard Essex accent, which no way could be mistaken for anything other than English.

"Sorry we have to check all scooters leaving Hastings." The policeman said apologetically, and waved them on, much to the relief of all four of them.

The two scooters stopped for a couple of minutes near Hurstmonceux, just to stretch their legs.

"Enjoying the throbbing power of the 125cc?" Stu asked the Parka-clad Rocker.

"Gutless fucking hairdryer." He replied with some feeling.

"And you let your mate ride your Gold Star?" Stu asked rather tactlessly.

"Don't remind me, I just hope he gets to Hailsham with bending it."

"I got me an AJS 500 as well as this GS which makes life interesting for a Mod in Hastings and just to add to that my girlfriend is a Rocker with a 200cc Tiger Cub, so you see your position ain't that bizarre."

"You got a motorbike?" The girl called Razzle asked Sandra."

"Yeah, you know what it is like depending on guys to take you everywhere, the bike gives me independence, I go where I want, when I want."

"But you are on the back of a scooter with a Mod, looking like a Mod."

"That's a long story, but he prefers me in tight leathers." Sandra joked.

"This place seems pretty fucked up, does everybody here live a duel life?"

"No, but it adds a bit a zest to life."

"Come on you girls stop chatting we have got to be somewhere."

Steve was already waiting at the rendezvous point in Hailsham as the two scooters pulled into the car park and looked up with relief when his scooter arrived in one piece.

"Rozzers stopped us in Little Common." Explained his friend Fred the Rocker from Southend, with a broad smile on his face, "But Razzle here soon persuaded them that she was not a Russian with some pretty colourful Anglo-Saxon expletives."

Over the next ten minutes all the scooters and motorbikes arrived and stood around as Nika made up her mind to hand herself in at the local police station.

Sandra nodded to a few of the Rockers she knew and watched their faces as they realised this little Mod bird was in fact one of them, Jim's sister.

"Does Jim know you are here with him?" One of the Rockers said pointing at Stu "He is a Mod."

"All part of the deception." She lied.

"Are you really going out with Sandra, that Rocker bird?" Fred asked.

Stu who shrugged his shoulders and nodded and looked over towards Sandra.

"Don't that make life difficult?" Fred inquired.

"It certainly adds another dimension to life, but it gives me great satisfaction to get on my motorbike again."

"I can understand that as he looked at the little red Vespa Sportique, but I don't think I could get used to riding that poxy little thing all the time. Shit, it is so slow you can watch the fucking grass grow."

"Why would you even think about it?"

"Quite fancy that Razzle." Fred said.

You Really Got Me – The Kinks

It was Tuesday morning; the Bank Holiday was over and Stu was riding his GS up Mount Pleasant towards Ore Village. He had already seen the newspaper headlines, 'The Second Battle of Hastings', 'Riot Police Fly To Seaside' and he smiled to himself thinking if they only knew half of it.

Paul's Bonnie was already parked up when Stu arrived at the garage and as he entered the workshop John beckoned him to the office, where he could already see Paul seated and beside him sat Mandy who without the heavy makeup he had seen her wearing before looked a hell of a lot younger than he first thought.

"I want you to meet Mandy who will be joining us as a receptionist and secretary."

"Joining us?"

"Yes." Replied John, "Paul here has talked me into it, she knows the garage business inside out as her old man used to run a successful garage in Balham before he was driven out of business by the same bastards that were screwing me."

"And she can strip an SU carb in the dark." Boasted Paul.

"I often wondered what you got up to at night." Stu remarked with an exaggerated stage wink.

"I know what you two did for me last weekend. How you planned it and carried it out is beyond me, but it has given me a new lease on life and I am not going to fuck it up this time." John explained and handed both Stu and Paul a little brown sealed envelope, "And this is my way of saying thanks. Now you get back to work, we got a Hillman Imp Californian coming in for an engine overhaul, a Morris Minor for a new clutch."

"Fifty quid." Stu said out loud as he opened the envelope, "That's a fucking fortune."

"Seems the Boss was happy with the outcome of our little adventure."

"And you and Mandy. Christ, you only met her a day or so ago."

"I know, we just clicked, she has had a shit life and this is a new start for her, and she decided to move into my flat with me."

"Jesus that's pretty fast going."

"I think you know right away when you have met the right girl, a bit like you and Sandra from what I hear from Jim, she has totally fallen for you. That little tomboy has turned into a feisty young woman."

"Tell me about it."

"Come on you two I don't pay you to stand and chat." Shouted John from the office.

"Some things don't change." Paul noted out loud, "Heads or tails who gets that fucking clapped out Hillman Imp."

Stu sat on his GS looking out to sea on the old tram turnaround in front of the Cooden Beach Hotel as he waited for Sandra to finish for the day. He was deep in thought as he suddenly heard footsteps behind him and turned to see Sandra.

"Hi Little Rocker bird."

"Don't you Rocker bird me you pouncey Mod. Get that souped-up hairdryer started and take me home."

Stu kick-started the Vespa into life and set off feeling Sandra's arms around him and that felt good.

If he thought he had had enough shocks for one day he was in for a further one when they went into Sandra's house and found sitting in the front room Sarah, one of the original Mod girls from Hastings.

"What are you doing here?" Sandra demanded.

"Jim invited me."

"Jim?"

"You know your brother."

"But...." Sandra started but words failed her.

"I met him through my sister who he went to school with him, and she said that he wasn't a bad type."

"But you are a Mod and he is a Rocker?" Sandra spluttered.

"Well you being a Rocker hasn't stopped you with Stu here has it?

"It hasn't made it easy." Sandra admitted but added as an afterthought, "but interesting."

Jim appeared with two cups of coffee in his hands, a broad smile on his face.

"You are a dark horse." Sandra snorted in laughter.

"If you can't beat then join them, if my little sis can make it work there is hope for me."

"How the fuck are we gonna explain this to everyone as if things weren't complicated enough before." Stu concluded.

"What was it Ringo Starr answered when asked if he was a Mod or a Rocker?" Sandra asked.

"I'm a Mocker." Stu and Jim answered in unison.

Standing in the garden smoking a cigarette before he left for home he explained his plan to Sandra, "I'm gonna get me a flat, preferably a ground floor one with a small garden to keep the AJS and a scooter to get out from under the feet of my old man who keeps giving me grief."

"What about your mum, how would she feel about you leaving home?"

"Probably make her life easier, not having me old man going on at me all the time."

"Would there be room for my Tiger Cub as well?"

"I am sure I can find a space for that and I'll even invest in a double bed if you want to join me."

"Is that a marriage proposal?"

"Well it's as near as you are gonna get before I speak with your dad."

Bird's Eye View (Razzle's Story)

Pamela Haswell was a Southend-on-Sea Mod, known to her friends as 'Razzle' for longer than she could remember and with her own scooter she knew that the August Bank Holiday was on the horizon and she would not miss this one having missed Clacton and Margate.

Harbouring a crush for one of her group she hoped this weekend would give her the opportunity to finally get him to notice her.

Walk On By- Dionne Warwick

Pam just stood in front of her full-length mirror and looked at the reflected image as if she was sussing out who or what was this girl who was standing in her bra and knickers.

Five foot five in her stocking feet, brown eyes with and dark brown hair that framed her face practically touching her shoulders, which at the moment was Sellotaped under her chin to encourage it to curl under.

"Don't need tissues to pad out me bra anymore." She thought to herself with a smile as she ran her hands over her boobs, then down over her flat stomach.

"Am I so bloody ugly that stuck up prick James went off with that slag Karen?" Pam asked the reflection of herself, "What has she got that I haven't?"

"Well she's got James." Pam said to herself, "Probably he found it easier to get into her fucking knickers than mine. Good luck to him, he ain't the fucking first that's for sure to get between her legs."

Pam walked over to the window, peered at the sky which looked clear, then at the shed where she kept her Vespa that she was so proud of and to have the independence of her own wheels, OK, the little white 125 Vespa Sportique wasn't the newest scooter, but it was hers and that gave her the freedom to do what she wanted, not just to wait for some fucking plonker to ask her out for a ride and then try it on or to be carried around like a trophy like on James' brand new GS 160, who thought more of his scooter that he did of any girl. Bastard.

"What was it with blokes and scooters?" Pam asked herself, "After all it was only a means of going from A to B for short distances, anything over twenty miles and they took the train so they didn't crease their fucking parallels."

Pam wondered who would be down the Dog tonight, probably Steve and Bandy Malc, they were always down there, usually playing poker dice for hours on end, Marshy, Big Ron and Mike Smith who was kind of cute but had a crappy clapped out scooter, with more rust on it than hers. Not the greatest choice of blokes in the world, but better than some of the types that hung around down at the Shades, who thought they were all high numbers.

It had been a long day behind the counter in Woolies, but she had been paid and had a couple of quid in her purse in case none of the blokes offered to buy her a drink.

Sitting doing her eyes, Pam decided on the big build up for tonight, starting with a dark brown line etched with brown eye liner and a brush in the crease of her lids, then a thin line of black eye liner very close to her eye lids. The eye lashes come next, fixative applied then bending the double thick lashes to fit the curvature of her eye lids, then finally black mascara on her lower eye lashes, sketched lightly at first then darkened. Beige foundation, a fluff of rouge and a little lipstick and a dab of perfume. "C'est ça »

At least her bloody period was over for another month which would have been a royal pain in the arse for the Bank Holiday Weekend, something less to worry about if she went off somewhere. She had come-on last weekend pissing off James and probably why he fucked off with Karen. What had she heard Steve call Karen? Oh Yes, 'the village bicycle. ridden by all the local boys'.

"What to wear?" Pam pondered out loud, as she picked up the blue wool jumper which had cost her two quid and held it up against herself, "That'll do and the grey tweed skirt."

Her best friend Val Shapland told her that she was looking more and more like Cathy McGowan, not really a true mod look as she had long hair, but Pam was OK with that, "If I like my fucking hair long I will have it long." She had responded to the jibe.

Ready Steady Go was required viewing on a Friday night, not just for the music but what was 'in' this week as the audience were all brought in from the local clubs in London. It also gave Pam the chance to see the latest dance moves.

"Right, that's it, polished and ready to go." She told the image in the mirror.

Anyone Who Had A Heart-Cilla Black.

Descending into the gloom and cigarette smoke down the stairs of the Harold Dog, Pam could see Steve and Bandy Malc over on their usual table, continuing their endless games of poker dice, seeming oblivious to the new arrivals.

Marshy and Mike spotted the two girls and called them over, "Come 'ere Razzle, got a couple of places here."

"Will I never lose this bloody nickname." Pam whispered to Val.

"Everyone knows you as Razzle. That's it, Pamela Haswell is Razzle."

"Don't even know how it started."

"Well you're stuck with it now."

Looking across at Steve, trying to catch his eye, but to no avail, she returned her gaze to Mike, a nice enough guy but she would have preferred to be chatted up by the one she really fancied.

"So how is that old scooter of yours?" Mike asked trying to break into the conversation.

Razzle looked at him and shook her head, "Is that your best chat up line?"

"Didn't think 'What's a nice girl like you doing in a place like this?' would have gone down that well."

"Has it ever worked before?" Razzle asked sarcastically.

Mike shook his head and laughed, "No."

"Well it wouldn't have worked on me either, and yes my Sportique is just fine and by the look of that wreck outside I would guess that old heap is on its last legs."

"I brought it off Steve."

"And I bet he told you that it only had one careful owner but he probably omitted the ten less than careful owners."

"It gets me from A to B." Mike said defensively.

"Eventually." Razzle added.

Down the stairs into the basement everyone noted the arrival of Big Ron Nicholson, "You heard the latest? The word has filtered down from the Smoke that Hastings is on for the August Bank Holiday next weekend."

Bandy Malc stood up and shouted over Green Onions by Booker T and the MG's blasting away on the juke box, "Now pin back your lug-holes and take note, it's 'astings next weekend, so get your glad rags ready we are going to the seaside."

"Make a change from Clacton and Margate." Said Mike Smith.

"Are you going to go?" Razzle asked.

"Yeah. Should be fun. Wanna come with me?"

Razzle looked at Val, before answering, "Yeah OK."

"So, we all meet up at about 8:30 on Saturday morning. I reckon it will take about two and a half hours. Up to the new Dartford tunnel, down to Maidstone, then across country to Hastings. That's the way I went before and it should be a clear run." Steve postulated.

"Sounds good to me." Bandy Malc said.

"And that goes for the rest of us." Said Big Ron, gaining nods from the others.

"Do you reckon that old 125 will make it to Hastings?" Razzle inquired.

"Can't see why not." Mike said with a confidence that he did not really believe.

"We could take my Sportique." Suggested Razzle.

"What a bird riding and a bloke on pillion. That would not do my credibility any good."

"You ride that wreck around town and you think that would damage your credibility? What about my credibility?"

"But you're a girl?"

"My God you are really with it tonight, your powers of observation sometimes just astound me."

"No, I didn't mean it like that." Protested Mike.

"I would stop there before I kick you in the balls and tell you to stick your offer where the sun don't shine."

"I'll get it checked over before next weekend."

"And I hope that includes not just counting how many fucking wheels the scooter has, but ensuring the battery is charged up, spark plug checked, fuelled up and polished to within an inch of its life." Razzle demanded.

Mike nodded furiously only too pleased that Razzle had unexpectedly accepted his offer.

While Mike went off to buy the girls a coffee, Val turned to Razzle, "Are you really going to Hastings with Mike?"

"I missed Margate and Clacton because me mum and dad wouldn't let me go by myself and as I have had no other offers, why not?

"You're crazy. What about James?"

"Fuck James."

"But do you even fancy Mike?"

Razzle looked across at Steve and his mates discussing the forthcoming adventure, "Didn't have any better offers, and he ain't so bad and you never know what can happen. Could be fun."

"You can always tell your parents you are staying at mine for the weekend." Val added providing Razzle with the perfect alibi.

"You ain't gonna go?"

"Nah, gonna have to look after my sister's little brat next weekend while they go away, I promised her, and in any case, you could end up sleeping rough on the beach, me I prefer a soft bed."

"I'll take my one-girl sleeping bag to protect my modesty, I ain't in the mood to have Mike pawing at me all weekend."

"But he is going to expect something for taking you down to the South Coast."

"What he expects and what he is gonna get is a completely different thing. Now if it had been Steve asking me, then it might have turned out differently."

"Do you still have the hots for Steve ?"

"Have for a long time but he never seems to notice me."

"Hear he split up with that bird from Rayleigh when his scooter broke down and she walked off."

"That's the bloody scooter he sold to Mike, a real rust bucket."

"You never know your luck, don't give up girl you might manage to catch his eye this weekend in Hastings."

"But I'm going with Mike."

"Don't mean you have to come back with him."

Shout-Lulu

Razzle stubbed out her second cigarette as she waited for Mike to arrive, her temper rising and cursing the fact that she could have taken her own Vespa.

From her catalogue she had ordered new slacks and jumper, which were now under her Parka and scarf wound around her neck. A small bag contained everything she would need for the next couple of days, and her sleeping bag rolled up tight.

She heard Mike's scooter before he came around the corner, picked up her things and walked to the curb, "Where the fuck have you been? I've been waiting here for fucking ages."

"Wouldn't start." Explained Mike, the embarrassment evident on his face.

"Bloody piece of junk. If it don't get us to Hastings I will bloody kill you."

"It's OK now, just a bit temperamental first thing in the morning."

"A bit like me then." Razzle added as she pushed the sleeping bag against the upright seat back on the pillion seat before climbing on.

With a look of achievement Mike kicked the one-two-five into life, first time, jumped on, kicked the stand back and accelerated away towards the assembly point at the Southend Victoria Circus roundabout, acutely aware that they were already running late.

By the time Mike and Razzle arrived, Big Ron and Marshy on their Lambretta's, Steve and Bandy Malc were there and waiting.

Razzle dismounted and went over to Steve's red Sportique, a model similar to her own. "Ain't had enough cash to do much to it yet." He admitted.

"Just love the colour, looks better in wine red than my one in white." Razzle commented running her hand over the double saddle.

"Not many birds have their own scooters."

"Can't let you lads have all the fun."

"So why are you here with Mike on that old one-two-five?"

"He asked me to come with him to Hastings, and against my better judgement I said yes, and it would have been the longest trip I would have made alone on my Vespa." Steve looked at his old Vespa and smiled, "May look like a pile of shit but it should get there."

"And that from the man who sold it to him." laughed Razzle.

"Got some hearts if you need 'em." Steve said patting the pocket of his Parka.

Bandy Malc was showing off his chromed side panels to the envy of the others, plus the six mirrors and the four spotlights he had added, "Cost me half-a-crown a square inch to have them chromed."

"Are we ready to roll?" Steve called out as cigarettes were stubbed out and the group climbed aboard their machines.

"The weekend starts here. Let 'em roll." Cried out Big Ron as he gunned his Lambretta onto the road with the others soon on his tail, with Mike and Razzle bringing up the rear.

"Give it some stick or we'll lose them." Shouted Razzle.

"It's alright for them, they ain't got passengers." Mike replied defensively.

"Well that's not my fault, it was you who asked me."

It was late morning as Mike and Razzle pulled into the car park at the Royal Oak Hotel in Hawkhurst, their numbers bolstered by about thirty other Mods on their scooters from Maidstone and Medway making their way to the coast.

Guests arriving at the hotel eyed the recent arrivals with a mixture of loathing and trepidation, and expecting trouble to break out at any moment.

Razzle was bursting for a pee and pushed her way into the hotel looking for the loo.

Playing catch-up for most of the journey down Mike had gunned the life out of the old one-two-five to try and keep up in what seemed a losing battle.

Relieved Razzle returned to the car park just to see Steve ride off alone.

"Where's he going?" She asked.

"His grandad and grandma live just down the road so he is off to say 'Hi' to them before catching up with us in Hastings. He reckons to meet up with us near a place called The Memorial in the centre of Hastings town, some sort of clock tower.

"He seems to know the town pretty well." Razzle commented.

"Yeah, he used to come down here when he was a nipper with his mum and dad." Explained Bandy Malc.

"It's only about seventeen miles." One of the Maidstone Mods answered hearing the conversation, "The clock tower is right in the centre of Hastings, you can't miss it.

"What's Hastings like?"

"Much like any other seaside town down on the south coast, not as big a Brighton, but some great fish and chip shops down the Old Town."

"I'm bloody starving, me stomach thinks me throat has been cut." Said Mike, realising that he hadn't eaten since breakfast.

"You have such a way with words." Razzle quipped sarcastically.

Mike looked at his riding companion standing there not fazed by all the Mods around her, well able to hold her own with a confidence even in this mostly male dominated group, "Don't you ever wish you were a bloke?"

Razzle looked at him realising how intimidating she must sound at times before answering him, "Never really thought about it, I am what I am. Can't change that. Don't think having a prick would make me a better person."

"Well for one I am bloody pleased about that." Mike said.

"Just get on yer scooter and take me to fucking Hastings."

I Only Want To Be With You- Dusty Springfield

As the small group travelled south more scooters were coming together until by the time joined the A21 at Sedlescombe, the whole road was filled with Lambretta's and Vespa's all heading in one direction towards the coast.

"Never seen so many Mods." Cried Razzle in exhilaration of the moment.

"Not seen one Rocker yet. Maybe they all stayed at home." Shouted Mike above the sounds of revving engines.

"Do you think there will be any trouble?"

"Probably, always some who want a bundle especially some of them fucking London Mods, if there are no Rockers then they will fight with anyone."

"Where we gonna stay?" Razzle asked.

"If it is anything like Margate all the hotels and B&B's will be full and have their doors shut to Mods."

"What was it like at Margate?"

"Mostly boring, bit of running about chasing a few Rockers before the coppers stepped in and attempted to keep us apart."

"My mum and dad wouldn't let me go after what they read about Clacton."

"But they were OK with you coming today?"

"Told them I was staying with Val to help look after Jamie, her sister's little one."

"Let's look for somewhere to park."

The friends all managed to park near each other up from the seafront past the large Hastings Observer building, "Cornwallis Gardens." Bandy Malc said as he spotted the street name, "The scooters should be alright here."

"And we passed that clock tower just down the road. Now we just have to wait for Steve." Said Mike.

As Razzle looked around her the whole town seemed to be packed by Mods, olive drab Parkas tucked under scooters to make the most of the good weather.

"So, where we gonna stay?" Razzle asked again.

"Dunno, maybe Steve will have an idea when he arrives, all I've seen so far is 'No Vacancy' signs in all the B&B's we've passed."

"Where did you stay in Margate?"

"Ended up sleeping rough under the pier, lucky the weather was OK not like fucking Clacton, fucking cold, fucking wet and fucking boring."

"Ain't that where we slept in that beach hut, the four of us and Steve's bird who was really pissed off." Bandy Malc added.

"Yeah, she chucked him didn't she, went off with some East London bastard in a car."

"Who was that?" Razzle asked.

"That little bird who worked in Boots the Chemist down the High Street, Shirley something."

"Not Shirley Smith, they used to call Smudger?" Razzle asked.

"Yeah, that's her."

"Steve don't seem to be that lucky with birds does he?" Razzle concluded, wondering why a good-looking bloke like him always seemed to be the one being dumped. She still hoped that one day he would ask her out and could judge for herself.

The Memorial appeared to be a meeting place for everybody, Mods everywhere.

"Keep your eyes open for Steve he should be here soon." Bandy Malc ordered.

"There he is." Shouted Razzle as she spotted him in the crowd.

"Where the fuck have you been?

We've been waiting for ages." Bemoaned Big Ron.

"Got a bit side-tracked, I want you to meet Nika."

"Leave him alone for a few hours and he turns up with the most gorgeous bird. How the fuck did he do that?" Marshy demanded.

Razzle looked long and hard at the girl, shoulder length black hair, which looked natural not out of a bottle, and clothes to die for. Where the hell did she appear from?

"Shit this girl has class, what the fuck does she see in you?" Razzle demanded.

"Sparkling personality, titillating conversation, her knight in shining armour." Steve boasted.

"Look at her shoes, this girl has all the latest fab gear." Declared Razzle.

"And she is Russian." Added Steve.

"Russian?" Mike questioned.

"Well she don't look Russian." Commented Big Ron.

"How would you know what a fucking Russian looks like?" Razzle fired back at him.

"I've seen that James Bond film and that Rosa Klebb bird and them Russian women athletes who look like they are built like brick shithouses."

"That hardly makes you an expert on Russian birds does it?" Razzle concluded.

"What language does she speak?" Marshy asked.

Nika turned towards him a big smile on her face, "Whatever language you like. French, German, English and Russian and I can get by in Spanish, so make your choice."

"We'll settle for English." Marshy concluded.

"Now let's get something to eat. Fish and chips from along the seafront by the fishing huts." Steve suggested.

"Sounds good to me." Answered Mike.

"Where the fuck did that girl come from?" Razzle demanded.

"Buggered if I know. Went off to see his grandparents and hey presto he appears with a bird in tow."

"Does he know her?"

"I have not the faintest idea, he never mentioned anything about picking up a bird to me." Mike explained.

To say that Razzle was jealous was an understatement, as her eyes burned into the back of the mystery girl. Why couldn't he have come back alone?

Walking across the road clasping their bags of fish and chips the friends tried to find some shade as the afternoon sun was now quite warm, the sudden sound stopped them dead in their tracks. A noise like rumbling thunder coming down the Old London Road, then they came into view, a hundred or more motorbikes riding four or five abreast.

As they passed the assembled Mods the abuse started, shouting and swearing emanating from both groups, but no attempt to stop them.

From the corner of her eye Razzle watched as a Mod she didn't recognise approached Steve whom it would appear he knew well.

"Hey everybody, this is Col a local Mod I met last year down here on holiday and he has offered his parent's place near that bloody great white building on the seafront for us to doss down tonight, anybody interested?"

Razzle poked Mike in the ribs and answered, "Yeah we will, I don't fancy sleeping under the pier on those fucking hard pebbles."

"Where you all parked up?"

"Cornwallis something?" Replied Mike.

"Cornwallis Gardens?"

"Yeah, that's it."

"My mate Stu here will ride up there and take you the back way down to Undercliff Terrace where my parent's place is, but luckily for us they are away for a few days so it's open house."

The girl with Stu looked at Razzle, and like her was dressed in high street clothes, unlike the Russian bird who was in obviously designer gear, "Seems we shop from the same catalogue." She said with a winning smile, "My name is Sandra. Welcome to fucking Hastings."

Just One Look-Doris Troy

Mike and Razzle followed Stu and Sandra across St Leonards until they reached the enormous white building that looked similar to a nineteen thirties steamship-like super structure.

The front door was half open as they approached the terraced cottage, to be met by a short haired blond girl.

"Col sent us and said that Mike and his girlfriend could stay here, rather than tough it out on the beach." Sandra said in the way of an introduction.

"Come on in, make yourselves at home." Linda indicated as she opened the door wider.

"They are friends of Steve from Southend." Sandra explained.

"Toilet is up on the first floor if you wanna freshen up, help yourself to a coffee if you want."

"Dying for a piss, it's OK for the blokes they can piss anywhere if you know what I mean."

"Like marking their territory." Laughed Linda.

Behind them Col arrived and went through to the kitchen.

"Fancy a fag over on the promenade across the road?" asked Sandra as Razzle reappeared form the toilet.

"Why not, at least you got the sea here rather than one and half miles of mud in the Thames Estuary."

"You don't make it sound that exciting."

"It ain't compared to this."

"Did I hear Mike say that you had your own scooter. A Vespa." Sandra asked.

"Yeah, but I came down on the back of a clapped out one-two-five."

"I ride as well, got meself a bike."

"A bike?"

Sandra hesitated realising what she had said, a 200cc Tiger Cub."

"But that's a motorbike."

"Wasn't always a Mod, in fact I still ain't a proper Mod. I prefer me leathers rather than this gear, but Stu is a Mod and I cross over between the two."

"You're a Rocker?" Razzle said in astonishment, "Yeah, but you look like a real Mod."

"It's only clothes that make me a Mod, I prefer the wind in my face and the independence my bike gives me, but that's OK with Stu."

"So, is it true that Rocker birds use Duckhams 20/50 motor oil instead of KY Jelly?" Razzle joked.

"Yeah, have to keep it oiled up for you never know when you're gonna need it, in any case they say Essex girls carry their knickers in their handbags."

"Saves time don't it." Razzle admitted a huge smile across her face.

The two girls looked at each other and burst into a fit of giggles, they had more in common than the clothes they were wearing.

"That sounds like Steve's Sportique." Said Razzle as she turned to watch Steve park his scooter and walk up to the front door. Razzle and Sandra re-crossed the road and joined them on the steps. As Steve pushed the half open front door back he was confronted by Linda who glared at the newcomers.

"Colin invited us, my name is Steve and this is Nika."

"It's alright Linda, they are friends." Came Col's voice from the kitchen.

"Is she the Russian bird you talked about?" asked Linda turning to Col who had come out into the hallway.

"Excuse Linda, she is half Polish and has no great love for the Russians."

"Przepraszam, że nie chcę cię obrazić" Said Nika.

"You speak Polish?" Linda said in surprise.

"Just a little." Admitted Nika.

"Wejdź."

Steve looked in amazement at Nika's linguistic skills, "I thought you said that you only spoke. French, German, English and Russian and a little Spanish?"

"And also, some Polish." She giggled.

"Grab a beer and make yourself comfortable." Col offered as went into the front room and sank back onto the settee and joined by Linda, "Looks like everything is gonna heat up tomorrow. Loads of Rockers are still pouring into the town,"

Razzle looked across at Nika who had hardly spoken since she arrived, "Are you alright luv?"

"I'm not used to this beer, it tastes strange."

"She is Russian so she probably wants a Vodka." Quipped Linda.

"I think the old man has a bottle in his drinks cabinet, I remember seeing it at Christmas. Ah here it is, Cossack Vodka." Col said as he half-filled a tumbler and handed it to Nika, who sniffed it before downing it in one gulp.

"Think the girl has a bit of a thirst on her. Give her another." Razzle demanded.

"So where did you meet Steve?" Razzle asked the question everybody wanted to know."

"He stopped an offered me a lift."

"Would you normally just accept a lift from a stranger?"

"He seemed different, not a threat and I was lost." Nika admitted.

"Lucky for you he is a genuine guy, not something I would say about a lot of the boys."

"You like him?" Nika asked as she looked into Razzle's eyes.

"Yeah I quite fancy him."

"But you are not his girlfriend?"

"No, just a friend."

Nika finished the vodka in one gulp, understanding now why her mother found solace in the fiery liquid, it helped to calm her anxiety.

I Don't Know What To Do With Myself-Dusty Springfield

"You know the Rolling Stones are on the pier tonight? Do wanna go?" Col asked.
"Can you get tickets?
"Yeah, ten bob each." Col replied.
"Do wanna see the Stones? Steve turned towards Mike and Razzle who were both nodding as was Nika.
"Can you get four?"
"Can't see that will be a problem. I know the guys on the pier, they will get us in. leave it to me" Col answered confidently.
"Shame they got knocked off the number slot in the charts this week by the Beatles."
Razzle admitted even though the Stones were not a Mod group the song 'It's all over now' seemed to pretty much sum up her life.
"I saw the Beatles film 'A Hard Day's Night' in London." Nika said.
"Yeah, I saw it in Southend at the Odeon."
"No, I saw the Beatles at the World première of A Hard Day's Night at the London Pavilion in July."
"I saw that on television. Wasn't Princess Margaret there?"
"Loads of rich people were there, tickets cost fifteen guineas each." Nika added.
"Fuck me, that's a lot of money to see a film."
"It was for charity, My father brought the tickets for my mother and I."
"Is your ole man rich or something?"
Nike didn't respond to the question, but continued, "After the screening my mother and I went on with The Beatles, the royal party and other guests including The Rolling Stones to a supper party at the Dorchester Hotel."
"So, you actually saw the Beatles and Stones in person?"
Nika nodded.
"What does your father do then?" Razzle probed further.
"He works in London."
"Ain't you Russians supposed to be communists where everybody is equal?"
"Some people are just more equal than others." Nika said, the embarrassment clearly evident in her voice.

"Come get ready we gotta get down the pier to see the show." Said Col.
"You got tickets OK?"
"No problem. It's not what you know more who you know." Col said tapping the side of his nose.
Leaving their scooters, the three couples walked along the promenade towards the pier and it was soon obvious by the long queue that stretched from the 'The Happy Ballroom' all the way down to Bottle Alley that tonight was a sell-out.
"Don't worry about the queue, I got this worked out." Boasted Col, as they walked past the long line of fans, boosted in numbers because of the holiday weekend with out-of-towners who had taken advantage of the opportunity to see their heroes.
Near the front of the line Col halted his friends as he looked for someone.
"Here Col." Came the call from a tall Mod with his girlfriend, "Come and join us."

Even as they pushed into the line it was obvious that their intrusion was seriously pissing off those behind in the queue.

"You fucking can't just push in, we've been queuing for ages. Get the fuck out of it." Shouted one particular Mod, one that Steve knew, a workmate, well not a mate and his girlfriend who was the boss's daughter,

Mick the tall Mod turned and walked back towards mouthy complainant, the look on his face and his balled fists should have warned him that his intentions were far from friendly.

"You got a problem arsehole?"

"This is a fucking queue, you just can't let these people push in."

"These are my friends, and I was saving a place for them. Understand?"

"Even him?" The mod pointed towards Steve."

Mick turned and looked back at Steve and Nika, winked and turned back face to face.

"As I said, I was saving a place for my friends, is there something in that statement you have difficulty in understanding?"

Realising that any further discussion was going to end up in violence the mod took the line of least resistance and shut up.

Turning to others in the queue Mick simply asked, "Anyone else got a problem with me mates joining me?"

The shuffling of feet and downward cast eyes seemed to indicate that nobody else was willing to take up the challenge.

"Ain't that Paul and Pamela from the Shades?" Razzle demanded.

"Yeah, that stuck up cow's old man owns the picture framing company Steve works for, and that Paul who thinks he is a real Ace Face is a total wanker." If Pamela had known what was good for her she would have shut up, but that was her problem she just didn't know when to button it, "Look at her, common little slut, dressed like a common tart." She said within the hearing of Razzle to whom the jibe was intended.

Razzle turned, her anger rising as she walked back down the queue to confront the source of the abuse, "You talkin' to me?"

Looking to the right and left then at Razzle she laughed, "Can't see anybody else that fits that description, a stupid little Woolies shop girl."

"At least I have got my own teeth." Razzle retorted.

"What is that fucking supposed to mean?" Pamela sneered.

"If you don't shut the fuck up you will be taking your teeth home in a bag."

"You can't talk to me like that."

"So, what you gonna do about it?"

At last the message got home and Pamela stood back, one look at Razzle was enough to convince her she was not joking.

Sandra now joined Razzle seeing the confrontation, "This cow giving you some grief?" she asked.

"No, it's OK, I think she has got the message that if she don't keep her gob shut, she won't be eating solids until she has a set of dentures made and if he makes any trouble for Steve," Razzle said pointing at Paul, "I will take it personally, and come looking for her"

"Come on you two the line has started to move." Called Col.

Razzle turned back to join Mike who had watched the whole performance, "Remind me not to piss you off." Mike concluded.

Dancing In The Streets-Martha And The Vandellas

Razzle was still buzzing with excitement as she walked back along the promenade, the Stones had been great and she felt the music go right through her.

"Fucking great." Razzle shouted out across the empty ocean, her body covered in sweat and a dampness she found difficult to explain from the performance, "Wished they could have played longer."

Steve walked hand in hand with Nika and looked happier than he had been for ages and Razzle wished them well in spite of her crush on him. even though she would have loved to swop places with the Russian bird.

"Seen the Stones twice here in Hastings and this was by far the best performance to date." Col added.

"Saw the Stones with the Everly Brothers and Bo Diddley last October at the Odeon in Southend." Steve added, "Bloody fantastic. I brought 'Come On' when I first heard it on Radio Luxemburg, just about summed up my life at the time." Steve admitted.

Razzle looked at Nika and then at Steve and added, "Well it looks like your luck has changed now."

It was the early hours before everybody decided to turn in, Col directed Razzle and Mike, then Steve and Nika into separate bedrooms upstairs,

"The bog is the last door on the right." Shouted Col from the hallway, "Don't do anything I wouldn't do."

"What are you fucking smiling at?" demanded Razzle, "You are fucking sleeping on the floor."

"But....?"

"But what? Razzle interjected.

"I thought we might get together." Mike said, half pleading, half hoping."

"Well you bloody thought wrong."

"It seems a shame to waste the whole bed."

"I am not wasting it, I'm sleeping in it." Razzle said with a finality that even Mike understood, "And turn the fucking light out I don't want you watching me undress."

From the next room Razzle could hear Steve and Nika making love and she fantasised it was her that he was fucking, as she fingered herself vigorously under the bedclothes enjoying the wetness between her legs.

"Come here." She whispered to Mike who stood up and moved over to the bed.

"Sort of makes you randy hearing them at it, don't it?"

"Just shut up and climb in beside me."

Razzle was aware that he had a hard on and was as excited as her, as he ran his hands over her hardened nipples then down across her stomach, stroking her pubes before pushing his hand between her legs.

Razzle spread her legs wide, her intention obvious, for him to enter her.

"If you cum inside me I will cut your fucking prick off."

"Didn't know you were a catholic." Mike said as he slipped inside her.

"I ain't a catholic, I don't want to get pregnant."

It was the sound from many high revving motorcycle engines that brought everybody in the house back to wakefulness.

"Well it looks like a whole load of Rockers have arrived, thought they might have stayed away."

"They have as much right to be here as us." Razzle reminded him.

"But we outnumber them ten to one, you would think they would go somewhere else."

Razzle pulled the bedclothes up under her chin and closed her eyes. She knew it had been a mistake to shag Mike but when needs must. He had satisfied her need and as threatened did manage to cum over her rather than in her. Not on the pill the threat of pregnancy is a pretty effective contraceptive and the last thing she wanted was that, curtailing her freedom and forcing her into marriage was not how she wanted to end up.

She decided then and there to go on the pill, everyone said that it was easy to get the doctor to put you on pill, you just had to say that your periods were irregular and painful and the GP would write out the prescription.

She heard Mike and Steve go downstairs and after going for a pee saw that Nika was sitting on the bed in the next room, and went in.

Nika looked up as Razzle entered, still just in her bra and panties.

"You OK?" Razzle asked and immediately noticed Nika's 'Peachy' dress hanging over the back of a chair and picking it up she had a good look at it, looking inside at the label, "It's a real Mary Quant, dress, shit that must have cost a fortune."

"Try it on, we are about the same size." Said Nika indicating the designer dress.

Razzle slipped the dress over her shoulders and looked at herself in the full-length bedroom mirror, a big smile across her face. "What I'd give for to own a dress like this, on my wages this is just a dream." She proclaimed.

"Then do me a swop, give me your slacks and top and we will call it a deal."

"But my stuff is just brought in the high street, it ain't designer labelled like this, are you sure?"

"It looks better on you than it did on me." Nika said as she watched Razzle turn around in front of the dressing table mirror with an ear to ear smile.

"It makes me feel like a million dollars." Razzle purred.

"You better have these." Nika said, as she handed Razzle her tights.

"Never had a pair of these before, always wore stockings and a fucking suspender belt."

"They are becoming all the rage with shorter skirts, don't think the men like them as much as stockings, but then they don't have to wear them and it stops them leering up your skirt."

Razzle stood back and turned to look in the mirror again and liked what she saw.

Every Little Bit Hurts-Brenda Holloway

For most of the morning and early afternoon the Mods and Rockers rode on their respective mounts around the town, while the police who seemed to be increasing in numbers all the time doing their best to keep them apart.

"I am bored, hungry and need a piss." Moaned Razzle as she endured the umpteenth circuit of the town.

"Could go to the chippy again by the fishing net huts on the seafront." Mike suggested.

"Sounds good to me and there are some bogs down there." Razzle replied.

Parking the scooter up in Harold Road, Razzle and Mike headed down to the seafront and the numerous fish and chip shops.

The seafront was packed with Mods everywhere enjoying the sunshine, eating 99's or bags of chips as Mike looked for his friends. There were so many bodies around it made searching difficult, but it was Razzle who spotted Mick the Mod who had kept a place for them on the previous evening who stood head and shoulders above a huddle of Mods over in the coach park. Nearby Bandy Malc and Marshy were tucking into a bag of chips and fighting off the persistent seagulls who were well adapted to plucking chips from their hands before they could get them in their mouths.

Razzle could also see Stu and Sandra plus Steve with Nika on his arm.

"Looks like the whole gang had the same idea." Joked Mike.

"Get me six penny worth of chips, I'm off for a slash, before I burst." Shouted Razzle as she headed off to the nearest ladies' toilet to spend a penny and it came as no surprise that there was a long queue. There was always a queue which there never seemed to be for the men's toilets.

Relieved in more ways than one, especially after getting out of the smelly cubicle Razzle found herself confronted by three girls, Pamela the mouthy cow from last night, her friend Janet White and the one they called Little Sue who was anything other than petite, all from Southend.

"Well if it ain't the Woolies slut. Mutton dressed as lamb in gear she probably stole." Cajoled Pamela.

Slowly the three girls surrounded Razzle making it impossible for her to keep an eye on all of them at once.

"So, what were you gonna do to me?" Pamela taunted the outnumbered Razzle.

"Knock you're fucking teeth out." Razzle replied.

"Well we will see about that."

Razzle never saw the first punch that hit her in the kidneys, followed by a fist driven into her stomach winding her and dropping her to her hands and knees.

Janet then put the proverbial boot in, kicking Razzle with as much force as she could muster up into Razzle's ribcage.

Little Sue was about to kick Razzle in face when she felt a sharp tap on her shoulder and as she turned her head she took the full force of Nika's foot against her head felling her like a sack of potatoes.

"Like the footwork Nika", Sandra said as she turned her attention to Janet who was now becoming aware that something had gone badly amiss. With a kick to the kneecap Janet went down screaming like a banshee, "Fucking bitches. Fuck you."

"Mouthy little cow ain't she, just don't know when to button it." Sandra noted.

Nika then stamped on her outstretched hand and kicked her in the face which seemed to deter any more abusive language.

Both Nika and Sandra now turned on Pamela.

"Don't you dare fucking touch me." Screamed Pamela.

"Wouldn't touch you with a barge pole, but I might smack you across the face with my fist.

"You touch me and my boyfriend will be cutting you up."

Nika just elbowed Pamela in the face, the sound of splintering cartilage echoing around the coach park, "Sorry got bored waiting." Nika smiled angelically.

"Where the hell did you learn those fancy kicks and moves, the KGB?" asked Sandra as she helped Razzle to her feet.

"No, another establishment equally as tough, the Cheltenham School for Young Ladies in our self-defence class to protect our chastity against unwelcome attention.

Razzle looked down at Pamela, her nose smashed and two front teeth at least missing and was desperately trying to staunch the flow of blood with a bloodied handkerchief.

"I warned you, but you just can't keep your fucking mouth shut, can you? Next time you will not get off so lightly." Razzle hissed through her teeth between bouts of shooting pains in her stomach.

A crowd of women surrounding the action had just had their worst fears confirmed, these Mods girls were animals, violent and dangerous, everything the papers had said confirmed before their very eyes.

As they returned to the boys Razzle spotted Paul over near the water's edge and called Mike over and pointed him out, "The mouthy Mod from last night will be out to cut you and Mick the Mod up when he finds out his girlfriend has come worse off in a fight when she and a couple of friends tried to do me over."

Mick the Mod turned, picked up a leg of a broken deck chair and walked purposely towards him with Mike beside him.

Not unduly worried by the appearance of two Mods making their way towards him, Paul waited patiently for his girlfriend and a couple of her mates to return.

"Seems like your bird has walked into something after trying to hurt our friend Razzle." Mike smiled without humour.

"What do you mean?"

"It would appear that her and her mates tried to beat up Razzle but ended up getting the worst of it, but Pamela then said that you were gonna cut Razzle up."

"That's a load of bollocks." Paul said reaching for his Stanley knife in his pocket.

He had no sooner got the knife out with Mick brought the deck chair leg down across his arm, breaking it with one blow.

"Watch out for my fucking suit you morons"

"Did you hear that more concerned about his suit than his bird."

"Don't suppose your suit is waterproof?" Mike asked.

"What the fuck are you talking about. You've broken my fucking arm now you ask if my suit is waterproof." Paul screamed in confusion.

"Might be a drip-dry suit." Laughed Mick the Mod as he a Mike manhandled the mouthy Mod into the sea with a giant push, sending him flying into the gently breaking surf.

"You should have seen Nika here, like one of them Russian agents from SMERCH in the James Bond films, dropped that bitch with a single kick to her head" Sandra explained as Razzle sat on a low wall getting her breath back.

"You did not do so bad yourself." Nika added.

"How you feeling?" Sandra inquired as she knelt beside Razzle, "After you left we saw them three bitches follow you and tagged on behind just in case of any aggro."

"Certainly, glad you did."

"Do you wanna go up to the hospital?" Sandra asked.

"Bit bruised that's all, don't think anything is broken although my ribs hurt like fuck."

By now the boys had gathered round and had been updated with the incident.

"They could make life difficult for you at work." Razzle said as she looked up at Steve.

"I don't intend to work there forever."

Baby I Need Your Loving-Four Tops

By mid-afternoon the police presence had become overwhelming with reinforcements having been flown in to Lydd Airport and others shipped over from Brighton.

"More like a police state than a seaside town, they have even got the fucking mounted cavalry here." Concluded Steve as he watched a mounted patrol near Robertson Street.

"Spoiling all the fun." Added Mick the Mod.

"We could go to the Pam Dor, my local coffee bar and work out what to do." Suggested Col.

"I remember that place, near the Memorial, upstairs by Burtons." Steve said, having visited it the previous year when on holiday in Hastings, "Bit like the Harold Dog but upstairs instead of down."

"Thought the cops were heavy handed in Margate but it don't compare with this." Mike recalling the previous Whitsun Bank Holiday Weekend."

"Pretty heavy in Brighton last Whitsun as well. "Stu added.

"Trying to take all the fun out of the Bank Holidays." Mike concluded.

The Pam Dor was crowded as the group climbed the steep staircase up to the coffee bar.

Razzle was pleased to be sitting again as her ribs ached from the kick she had sustained and ordered a coffee which arrived in a clear Pyrex cup.

"So? What we gonna do now?" Mike asked out loud above the music blaring from the juke box.

"Could call it a day and bugger off home." Big Ron added who had re-joined the group on the way back along the seafront.

The appearance of three girls who had just arrived through the smoke-filled gloom suddenly made the idea of leaving redundant as Bandy Malc switched into chat-up mode, "Hello darlings. Wanna a coffee?"

"It's alright Shirl, he is from Essex but is house trained I am reliably informed." Called Col to one of the girls.

"There's a party tonight up at house on the park, Upper Park Road, you know it?" shouted Shirl above the music.

"Sounds cool. You all going?"

"Yeah should be a good bash."

"Fancy going to a party?" Steve said as he turned to Nika then to Mike and Razzle, who all nodded in agreement.

"OK we will be up there later."

It was a large Victorian house and not difficult to find with all the parked scooters and music blaring out through the open windows.

Bandy Malc led the group up the front path with Shirl the girl he had picked up from the Pam Dor.

The big guy at the door did not seem the welcoming type as Bandy Malc tried to push through.

"No fucking gate crashers." He growled.

"It's alright we are friends of Sarah, we're invited." Explained Shirl, "Come on Bill. You know me, Colin and Linda here plus a couple of his mates, we don't mean no trouble."

"Well no trashing the joint."

The house was crammed full, the Dansette record player was cranked up to full volume in the front room where couples were shuffling to Louie Louie by the Kingsmen.

"Go help yourselves to some booze in the kitchen."

In the front room couples gyrated to the music as Razzle kicked off her shoes and joined Nika who was dancing alone.

"You OK?" Razzle asked above the music.

"I have never been to party like this before, my parents would never allow it."

"Most parents don't like the idea of their daughters coming to parties, with all these randy Mods around, if you know what I mean?"

"You like Steve, don't you?" Nika asked.

"Known him for some time but have never actually gone out with him, he is a nice guy. He seems to really like you." Razzle added.

"I've never met anybody like him." Nika admitted.

"Don't hurt him."

"I have to go home soon, and I doubt whether I will ever be able to see him again."

"London ain't that far."

"Here's some water." Steve announced as he fought his way through the smooching couples handing the glass to Nika to take a few uppers. You want any Razzle?"

"Won't say no. Need something to keep me going, take me mind of the kicking that cow White gave me." Razzle said as Steve tipped a few of the purple shaped tablets into her open hand.

"Just shout if you need any more."

"You seen Mike?"

"Yeah, out the back chatting up some bird."

"What a surprise." Razzle chuckled to herself, "Well good luck to him."

Wishin' & Hopin'-Dusty Springfield

Razzle saw Steve and Nika leave in the early hours of Monday morning, she was too high to care and Mike too pissed to ride his scooter, so they both crashed out at the party.

Mike looked the worst for wear after drinking much more than he initially intended and was now searching desperately for some aspirin and a cigarette.

"You got any smokes left?

"Nah, run out last night, gonna have to find a newsagent to buy some."

"You ready to go?"

Ready as I will ever be." Razzle mumbled, as she attempted to make herself look presentable. One look in the hall full length mirror instantly confirmed her worst fears, eyes red, make up smudged and clothes which looked like they had been slept in which of course they had.

"Where's the nearest ciggie shop?" Mike demanded of another early riser.

"Beaney's down the Battle Road."

"Thanks. That'll do."

The tatty Vespa started at the first kick, which in its self was a miracle and the set off up towards Silverhill to find Battle Road.

Razzle leant on the scooter chewing her nail in anticipation of her first cigarette as Mike went into the shop.

Bursting out of the shop, clutching a newspaper he seemed suddenly animated, "Look at this." Mike demanded.

"Why would I want to read the Daily Mirror, I need a cigarette."

"But you gotta see this. Look Here." Mike said pointing at the page.

Through bleary eyes razzle followed his finger to the page headlines, RIOT POLICE FLY TO SEASIDE. "So?"

"No here, it's that Russian bird, she is Russian diplomat's daughter and has gone missing or been abducted and there is a massive police search for her."

Razzle peered at the photo of a girl, somewhat younger than the Nika she knew, but defiantly the same girl.

"Bloody Hell. What the fuck is she doing here?"

"Dunno but we gotta get down to Col's house to let them know."

Forgetting the need for their nicotine fix they mounted the old one-two-five and headed off to the seafront.

The frantic raping on the front door soon brought everybody awake and Steve could hear Mike down in the hallway. Something was wrong.

"What's happened?" Steve shouted as he came down the stairs.

"Look at this." Mike said holding up the newspaper.

Steve scanned the Daily Mirror headlines, 'Riot Police Fly To Seaside'

"That explains all the coppers."

"No, not that read further down and look at the photo."

Staring out from the page was a photo of a younger Nika and below the caption, 'Russian Diplomat's daughter abducted in Kent. Nika Petrova went missing on Saturday around midday and police are conducting searches to find her. Reports that she was seen riding on the back of a scooter in the direction of Hastings have not been confirmed, but investigations continue'.

"Jesus Fucking Christ. What the fuck is going on here?" cried Steve.

From the top of the stairs dressed only in a pair of knickers and Steve's Ben Sherman shirt, Nika stood, tears in her eyes.

"Is this true? Are you this diplomat's daughter?"

Nika lowered her eyes and nodded.

"What the fuck was a Russian Diplomat's daughter doing wandering around in Hawkhurst?" Steve demanded.

"There is a secret Russian Embassy residence at Flimwell, Seacox House, where diplomats and Embassy staff can take time out from London. The KGB look after security and the American CIA keep an eye on who comes and goes." Nika explained.

"This sounds like a fucking James Bond film with KGB and CIA involved."

"I was so bored and when I said that I escaped I was telling the truth. I went out for a walk in the grounds and got out through a gap in the perimeter fence, without being seen, and when I passed a couple of Americans up near the main road, they just wolf-whistled and made some obscene suggestions. So, I just kept walking and that is when I met you."

"Didn't you realize what trouble you could get into, and for that matter the deep shit that I am now in?"

"It would be hard for you to understand what my life was like. I had no freedom. If I went shopping I had a KGB minder. At Cheltenham College for Young Ladies, I was kept separate from the other girls except for lessons and watched all the time. I had no life. You have freedom to do want you want. I envy girls like Razzle, she has a life."

"And now what do we do?" Steve demanded.

"I think I will have to go back." Nika said her head bowed, a tear in her eye.

Razzle put her arm around Nika's shoulder and held her close, feeling her shaking with fear, "Did you realise what would happen if you ran away?"

"I just needed to get away, anywhere to see what life was really like, and then Steve came along on his scooter and I saw my opportunity."

"But that could have been dangerous, just getting picked up by anybody don't you understand that?"

"I did not feel threatened by Steve, he seemed so open and now I have met all of his friends I can see my judgement was right."

"But if Steve is caught he could end up in prison, who is going to believe a Mod."

"I promise that Steve will not be implicated or any of you."

You'll Never Walk Alone-The Blue Bells

By midday the whole group had assembled at Col's parent's house at Undercliff Terrace and now knowing the whole story tried to work out a solution.

Nika sat with Razzle's arm around her, continuing to try and comfort her.

"The police are herding up all the Mods and attempting to march them out town in small groups towards Rye, which gives them the opportunity to get a good look at everyone, so we need to avoid un-necessary attention. We need some kind of plan to get Nika out of town without being spotted." Explained Steve.

For the next half hour everyone made suggestions including getting her onto a train or bus or even walking along the seafront to Bexhill.

It was Sandra who made the obvious statement that the police were not looking for a Rocker and Steve immediately liked the idea. His friend from Southend was in the enemy camp, Fred had come down on his BSA Gold Star and knew that he could depend on him if he could find him.

Razzle watched as Steve set off on his red Sportique towards the open-air bathing pool in St Leonards with a white pillow case tied to his whip aerial.

It was where it was rumoured there were a number of Rockers and where he hoped to find his friend.

Now the only thing everybody could do was wait.

"Sandra joined Razzle on the step for a cigarette, "If my brother is around he would help as well as he is a Rocker."

"What does your brother think about you going out with a Mod?"

Sandra laughed, "It's a long story, but he has accepted it, especially when he turned up at my place on his old AJS 500."

"A mod on a motorbike?"

"Well not exactly as a Mod as Stu still had his old leathers that he used to wear before his brought his first scooter and became a Mod and donned a Parka."

"This gets more intriguing by the moment." Razzle concluded.

"It certainly added a bit of spice to life, like living a dual existence."

"So how did you meet?"

"It was at Brighton last Whitsun, I badly cut my foot while I was paddling in the sea and he ran into the water to help me."

"But you said that you were a Rocker."

"Wasn't wearing much when I was in the water, it was only when Linda, Col's girlfriend found my leathers that my identity was exposed, but that didn't matter to Stu who took me to the hospital to get my foot stitched up. The rest is history."

"And I thought my life was complicated." Admitted Razzle.

It was the sound of Steve's scooter returning that ended the conversation.

Steve gathered the group around him and told them of his plan.

"And the Rockers agreed?" Bandy Malc asked.

"Luckily Fred was there so I had one friend in the enemy camp,"

"Why would you do all this for me?" Nika asked

"For the moment, you are one of us and that's enough."

"But why would the Rockers help me. I thought the Mods and Rockers were enemies."

"They are just like us really, they just happen to prefer fast motorbikes and most of what you read in the news rags is crap designed to sell more papers.

Yeah there are few that are out looking for a bit of aggro but mostly it's just about getting away with your mates for a couple of days having a bit of fun. Underneath that leather they have to go to work like the rest of us to earn a few bob. Any of us could just as easily become a Rocker, it's a way of expressing individuality."

"Basically, the plan is for Nika to leave Hastings on Fred's motorbike which I will be riding, both of us dressed in borrowed leathers and bone domes, while Fred rides my scooter." Steve said.

"I'll ride with your mate Fred if you like. I am the same build, similar colour hair as Nika and wearing her clothes who could tell us apart on the back of a scooter? Acting a bit like a decoy" said Razzle.

Steve looked at Razzle, impressed with her grasp of the situation, not just a pretty face but a feisty Mod girl that he knew he could depend on.

"And I have worked out a route for you to get out of town. Bexhill Road, De La Warr Road, then follow the Bexhill Hospital signs, then A269 to Ninfield the onto Hailsham. Then from there it's up to you." Col added.

"Sounds good." asked Steve.

"But what do you plan for Nika after we reach Hailsham?" asked Razzle.

"It will be up to Nika to decide what she wants to do, but once out of Hastings it will give her more options." Declared Steve.

Steve and Nika, Mike and Razzle, Stu and Sandra flanked by Bandy Malc, Big Ron and Marshy set off towards the Bathing Pool, to meet up with the Rockers. If they got stopped by the police now all the planning would be in jeopardy.

Fred was waiting for them as they brought their scooters to a halt with some thirty Rockers and their bikes waiting for them.

"This is Chrissy, Paul's girlfriend and she has agreed to lend Nika her leather jacket and crash helmet." Said Fred.

"She's a bit taller than me but it should fit OK." Chrissy noted but took off her jacket with some reluctance and handed it to the girl before her.

Nika put on the leathers and once her head was enclosed by the helmet she looked no different from any of the other Rocker birds.

As Steve and Fred swapped clothes a ripple of laughter and comments ran around the group, Fred now a Mod naturally receiving the majority of the ribald comments from his leather clad mates.

"Look after my scooter." Warned Steve as he helped Nika onto the back of the motorbike.

"I am more worried about you on something with more power than this souped-up hair dryer." Fred admitted.

"I'll look after it as if it were my own." Steve proclaimed.

"That's what worries me." Half-joked Fred.

"Now you know the plan, Fred here takes a hundred-yard lead then I swing in behind him with the other Rockers, the scooters then bringing up the rear-guard and block anything following us. Once we get to Bexhill Old Town and turn off for the hospital, Fred and Razzle with Stu and Sandra carry on towards Little Common and Eastbourne as a decoy, just in case we are followed. The Rockers stay with me riding shotgun until we all meet up at Hailsham at the church."

123

Bandy Malc keeps the scooters back in case we run into trouble. All clear?"

"Let's do it." Shouted Fred as he gunned the Vespa with full throttle towards the Bexhill Road.

Steve felt the throb of the 500cc engine beneath him as he twisted the throttle, gave it a few more seconds, flicked it into first gear and accelerated away feeling Nika's arms gripping him tightly around his waist.

To any bystanders, it was a hapless Mod being pursued by a gang of Rockers and the type of hooligan action they would expect from the youngsters.

Steve kept the distance behind Fred, but had to throttle back to ensure he did not catch up to him too quickly. Behind him the Rockers maintained position.

All went to plan and when Steve reached Bexhill Old Town he turned off to the right following the sign to the hospital, all was going to plan.

Once clear of Bexhill Steve opened up the BSA, bringing back a sense of speed he had not felt for a while on his Vespa and he had to admit it felt good.

When I Am Gone-Mary Wells

Razzle took one look at Steve's mate Fred and laughed, the sight of this Rocker with greased hair and wearing a Parka sitting astride a Vespa had really amused her.

"Watch it girl." Fred growled as she climbed onto the pillion seat, "I ain't gonna make a habit of this."

Pulling onto Bexhill Road with Stu and Sandra bringing up the rear they fell into the elaborate escape plan. They would ride through Bexhill and Little Common then cut up across country to join the rest at Hailsham.

It was Razzle who first noticed the police at the roundabout at Little Common stopping scooters and questioning their riders and passengers, especially if they were female. The policeman stood in the road with his had indicating the scooters stop, and indicated they pull into the kerb.

"Where are you heading?" The policeman asked.

"We are all off to Brighton." Sandra shouted, "Why are you stopping us we ain't done nothing wrong?"

"We are looking for a Russian girl with dark hair believed to be travelling on a scooter."

"There must be hundreds of girls that fit that description and we ain't Russian and my friend on the other scooter is from Essex, so you are wasting your time."

"Can't your friend speak for herself."

"Of course, I can fucking speak for myself, do I look or sound like a fucking Russian?" Razzle said in a hard Essex accent, which no way could be mistaken for anything other than English.

"Mind your language young lady, all I needed was a simple answer."

"Well we ain't Russian so can we go?"

"Sorry we have to check all scooters leaving Hastings." The policeman said apologetically, and waved them on, much to the relief of all four of them.

The two scooters stopped for a couple of minutes near Hurstmonceux, just to stretch their legs.

"Nearly pissed meself when that copper jumped out." Razzle admitted.

"Think you soon convinced him you weren't a Russki though." Sandra added with a smile.

"Didn't do my nerves any good either." Said Fred.

"Strange how just dressing differently can change how the world judges you." Said Stu.

"Lucky the copper didn't recognise me haircut is strictly non-Mod. Don't think he ever took his eyes of the girls, especially Razzle in that short skirt showing a bit of leg. Can't say I blame him."

"Even though she is a Mod?" Stu added.

"I don't care much for that shit, I ain't really a Rocker, I just happen to ride a motorbike and that's my passion.

"I can understand that, bikes get in your blood."

"But you are a Mod."

"I got me an AJS 500 as well as this GS which makes life interesting for a Mod in Hastings and just to add to that my girlfriend Sandra is a Rocker with a 200cc Tiger Cub, so you see your position ain't that bizarre."

"Fuck me. But, she is on the back of a scooter with a Mod, looking like a Mod."

"That's a long story, but he prefers me in tight leathers." Sandra joked and she joined in the conversation.

"This place seems pretty fucked up, does everybody here live a duel life?"

"No, but it adds a bit a zest to life."

Razzle felt pleased that their part of Steve's plan had gone OK, now it was time to see if he had succeeded.

"It's time to hit the road again." Ordered Razzle.

Steve was already waiting at the rendezvous point in Hailsham as the two scooters pulled into the car park and looked up with relief evident on his face when his scooter arrived in one piece.

"Rozzers stopped us in Little Common. But Razzle here soon persuaded them that she was not a Russian with some pretty colourful Anglo-Saxon expletives."

Over the next ten minutes all the scooters and motorbikes arrived and formed a circle around Nika

Steve turned to Nika and noticed she had that faraway look in her eyes, "You alright?"

"I've decided that I am going to hand myself in at the police station, so I think you and your friends had better make yourself scarce."

"I'll make up some story about getting a lift from a guy who thought I was a hitch hiker and then tried to get a bit amorous running his hand up my thigh, so he chucked me out of the car when I didn't respond to his advances and found myself lost in the middle of nowhere until I ended up here."

"Will your father believe that story?" Steve inquired.

"Would his little girl lie? Having to live rough and being frightened and alone in a strange country, plus a few tears. It will work. Look at my shoes scuffed and soiled, and wearing clothes I stole from a washing line."

"You are terrible."

Nika smiled and reached into her handbag, "And I want you to take this, so you can buy everyone here a drink for all of their help."

Steve looked at the wad of notes and whistled, "There must be a hundred quid here, I can't take that, that's more than fifteen week's wages."

"It was worth it. I have never had so much fun and I met you. It just a way of saying thanks."

"I don't want your money. I just want to know that you will be OK."

"Take it. My father wouldn't even miss it."

"Here I have written my address, write to me if you can." Said Steve handing her a scrap of paper.

"Walk me to the nearest police station, then get on your way back to Southend with your friends."

Steve watched as Nika pushed open the door of the police station, she turned and briefly smiled then went inside then he returned to the group.

Sandra nodded to a few of the Rockers she knew and watched their faces as they realised this little Mod bird was in fact one of them, Jim's sister.

"Does Jim know you are here with him?" One of the Rockers said pointing at Stu "He is a Mod."

"All part of the deception." She lied.

Razzle turned to Steve and put her hand on his shoulder, "Do you think that she will be alright?"

"I don't know. I hope so."

Steve then shared out the money Nika had given him it seemed the least he could do for all of their assistance.

"What you gonna do now?" Razzle asked.

"Probably go back up the A22 and head towards home. Wanna come back with me?"

Razzle looked across at Mike on his tatty one-two-five and turned back to Steve, "Yeah that'll be cool. Don't know if that old heap will make it back that far."

"Surprised it even made down here." Joked Steve.

The sudden appearance of a lone policeman on a Noddy Bike riding into the car park caught them all by surprise, not to mention a moment of panic for Steve.

Putting the bike up on its stand he walked across to the assorted group of Mods and Rockers, "Alright you lot move on, we don't want any trouble, here do we?"

"We ain't causing any trouble" Razzle responded.

"Al the same I want you to move on."

"Right officer."

Returning to their motorbikes and scooters the group split up to go their separate ways. Fred pleased to be back in his leathers and to have the power of his bike back again rather than the souped-up Singer sewing machine he had elected to ride here, kick started his BSA into life and headed off with the other Rockers.

The Mods with Razzle on the back of the Steve's red Sportique did a couple of circuits of the car park just to piss off the copper before setting off some back to Hastings the others to Southend.

The policeman just stood and watched convincing himself that he had successfully defused a serious situation from developing between these warring factions.

You're My World-Cilla Black

Razzle scoured the newspapers disregarding the lurid descriptions such as
ARRESTS REACH 70 AFTER HASTINGS CLASHES and POLICE MARCH GANG'S OUT
TO TOWN BOUNDARIES until she found the headline she was looking and hoping for.
 RUSSIAN DIPLOMAT'S DAUGHTER FOUND.

*Nika Petrov, the daughter of the Russian diplomat Alexandre Petrov walked into
Hailsham Police Station after having being abducted while holidaying in Kent.*

*Her abductor, a middle-aged man after unsuccessfully trying to molest her threw her out
of the car we believe near the Ashdown Forest where alone and frightened she
wandered for two days too afraid to approach anybody to help her in this country that
was so foreign to her. She apologised for stealing clothes off of a washing line when hers
became torn and dirty.*

Her mother and father were overjoyed at their daughters return.

*The Police are asking for any information concerning a green Austin A35 that the victim
described as her abductor's vehicle on Saturday 1st August, in or around the
Hawkhurst/Flimwell area.*

Initial reports that she was seen on a scooter have been discounted as coincidence.

Razzle reread the article twice and smiled to herself. Nika had promised to keep Steve
out of her story and she had. Good on the girl.

Razzle looked at her designer clothes on the bed, not washed yet but soon to be
cleaned and pressed so that she could show them off to her friends.

With the weekend behind her Razzle decided her Woolies days were over and she
would retake the Biology 'O' level she needed to make an application to become a
student nurse. She wanted to make something of her life not just selling jelly beans on
the sweet counter at Woolworths.

As for Steve that was another challenge. She had held on tight to him on the journey
back from Hastings and he had kissed her on the cheek when he had dropped her off
at her home. It was a start, a full bloody kiss with tongues would have been better but
from small acorns mighty oaks grow.

Those Were The Days My Friend- Mary Hopkin

It had been four years since that weekend in Hastings and much had changed in Razzle's life, including reverting to Pamela, her Mod days ended some years ago when she started as a student nurse in Southend General Hospital. Study and night shifts didn't go hand in hand with an active social life and when she went to bed it was to sleep.

Parking her trusty now ageing Vespa scooter she headed for Boots to buy some lippy and some other essentials before she started her next shift.

The last person in the world she ever expected to see was Steve walking towards her. After getting his exam, he had gone to work up in London and she had lost touch with him. She had gone out with Fred on a couple of occasions but it had not gone anywhere so she threw herself into her studying.

"Razzle?" Steve stuttered in disbelief, "Is that you?"

"Pam now." Razzle said pulling back her cardigan to reveal her name badge."

"Nurse Pamela Haswell SRN" Steve read out loud, "So you ain't just off to a fancy-dress party to play doctors and nurses."

"No, it's my fucking work gear you pervert."

"You got time for a coffee?"

Razzle looked at her fob watch and nodded, I ain't got long before I am on duty in Women's Orthopaedics with loads of old incontinent women with broken hips."

"That sounds like a shit job."

"Shit job is the right expression, bed pans all the time. Thankfully I have got an interview for a job at the Chelsea Hospital for Women working in A&E."

"I live in Chelsea, well nearly in Chelsea, I got a flat in Fulham and I work in Soho."

"Come on a let's get a coffee before you gotta go to work."

With two milky coffee's in front of them they hardly knew where to start.

"So, are you going out with one of these fine doctors?"

"Nah, try and keep work and pleasure separate. Jesus them docs are just randy buggers."

"Can't blame 'em seeing you in that uniform." Steve said with a mischievous glint in his eye.

"Fancy a girl in uniform, do you?" Razzle asked seductively.

"Always fancied you even back in the early days." Steve admitted

"But you never asked me out."

"You always seemed so self-assured, what with having your own scooter and everything."

"I wished you had." Razzle replied.

"So do I, but I always thought you would turn me down." Steve said.

"Whatever happened to the old gang?" Steve asked.

"That cow Karen White got up the duff with my old boyfriend and he had to marry her."

"Don't surprise me Leg-over-Lil was also good for a rumble."

"Bandy Malc using his head as God intended went to Oxford to read Theology, Marshy ended up on the photographic counter in Boots in Basildon, and Mike joined the police force. Don't know what happened to Big Ron."

"The whole scene changed after 1964, the Mod thing became so mainstream most the original Mods moved on." Steve reminisced.

"So, what about you?" Razzle asked.

"Got a job in an advertising agency, started sweeping the floors and am now in the graphics department working on adverts for the escalators for London Underground. Could be my big breakthrough if it goes well, but have to work strange hours with deadlines and things, so not a lot of time for socialising."

"So, you with anyone at the moment?" Razzle asked tentatively.

"Not really."

"We could meet up when I come to London for my interview next week." Razzle said hopefully.

"Best offer I have had in years." Steve admitted, "You could even stay over in my flat if you want to."

"That would be great." Razzle said and meant it.

Glossary of 60's language used in the story.

AJS: Motorcycles made by A. J. Stevens & Co. Ltd,

Beeza: Term for a BSA motorcycle.

Bird: Young usually attractive girl.

Black Bomber: Durophet capsules manufactured by Riker, that came in three strengths 20mg, 10mg and 5mg coloured black.

Black Maria: Police van used to transport prisoners after arrest.

Bob: Pre-decimal term for one shilling.

Bogs: slang for toilets (or restrooms)

Bone Dome: Crash helmet sometimes termed 'Skid Lid'.

Cathy McGowan: a British broadcaster and journalist, best known as presenter of the rock music television show, Ready Steady Go and In this role, she found herself suddenly propelled to fame as the symbolic new-profile 1960s teenager, casual in speech and manner, but dressed in creative fashions that made her popular with male and female viewers alike.

Chippy: Fish and Chip shop. Traditional English take away food restaurant.

Chuffed: Happy. (Dead Chuffed=Very Happy)

Clobber: Clothes.

Coppers, Rozzers and Plods: British Policeman.

Dansette Record Player: Was a British brand of mono record player manufactured by the London firm of J & A Margolin Ltd.

Drinamyl: Were a combined amphetamine/barbiturate that was commonly prescribed to women for anxiety and as a dietary aid. In the early to mid-sixties they could be obtained from dealers at nightclubs and were used by many Mods as a stimulant to keep them going through their all-night dancing sessions and known as Purple Hearts because of the shape of the tablet

Durex: The trademarked name for a range of condoms that were made in the United Kingdom by the London Rubber Company, known as 'rubbers' or 'johnnies'.

Fab: Pretty damn good.

Face (Ace Face) A face is a good mod; someone with the right clothes, the right haircut and the right taste in soul music and ska. An especially good mod would be an ace face or, more properly, The Ace Face.

Fags: Slang for cigarettes

French Blues: Amphetamine tablets-uppers.

Gaffer: Term used to indicate the boss of a company

Gear: Clothes.

Greaser: Another term for Rocker.

Guinea: Pre-decimal term for one pound one shilling or twenty-one shillings.

Half a Crown: Pre-decimal British coin and monetary unit equal to two shillings and sixpence, normally pronounced as 'two and six'.

High Number: See Number.

Miffed: Slightly pissed off.

Mod: A young person of a subculture characterized by a smart stylish appearance, the riding of motor scooters, and a liking for soul music.

Never-Never: Alternative name for hire purchase, popular in the 60's

Nifty: attractive or stylish.

Noddy Bike: Velocette LE (Little Engine) 149cc Police Motor bike

Number: A number was a run-of-the-mill mod, if you can imagine such a thing. Which when you bear in mind quite how special each mod considered himself to be, being considered just one of the herd was a stern insult indeed. But being classified as a high number was quite the compliment.

Pam Dor: Coffee bar in Hastings situated above a men's cloth shop.

Parallels: White trousers favoured by Mods.

Peachy: Excellent or attractive.

Purple Hearts: See Drinamyl.

Quid: Another term used for a British pound

Ready Steady Go: A British rock/pop music television programme broadcast every Friday evening from 9 August 1963 until 23 December 1966 on ITV, and gained the expression 'The Weekend Starts Here'.

Rocker: members of a biker sub-culture that originated in the United Kingdom during the 1950s. Often in the 20+ year-old age group.

Slash: Slang for a pee

Spend a penny: as above to go for a pee, a penny the cost to open the door.

Talent: A Mod girl or decent looking girl.

Ten Bob: From pre-decimal currency 'bob' = shilling and 20 shillings equals one British pound. A ten shilling note usually termed as ten bob note.

The Dog's Bollocks: The best.

(The) Smoke: Alternative name for London.

Ticket: A ticket is a bad Mod, someone still wearing last week's fashion, slightly grown-out hair, and not enough/too many mirrors on his scooter. It comes from third-class ticket, a reference to train fares.

Uppers: Stimulants (see Drinamyl).

Fact from fiction.

Mods and Rockers were two conflicting British youth subcultures of the early/mid 1960s. Media coverage of Mods and Rockers fighting in 1964 sparked a moral panic about British youth, and the two groups became widely perceived as violent, unruly troublemakers.

Newspapers described the Mod and Rocker clashes as being of "disastrous proportions", and labelled Mods and Rockers as "vermin" and "louts". Newspaper editorials fanned the flames of hysteria, which warned that Mods and Rockers were "internal enemies" in the UK who would "bring about disintegration of a nation's character". The magazine *Police Review* argued that the mods and rockers' purported lack of respect for law and order could cause violence to "surge and flame like a forest fire".

Eventually, when the media ran out of real fights to report, they would publish deceptive headlines, such as using a subheading "Violence", even when the article reported that there was no violence at all. Newspaper writers also began to associate Mods and Rockers with various social issues, such as teen pregnancy, contraceptives, amphetamines, and violence.

During the Second World War the use of stimulants was widespread throughout the armed forces to enable them to stay alert and to cope with long combat missions, By the early sixties It should be remembered that amphetamines were not illegal at that time in the United Kingdom, which fitted in perfectly with the ideal of clean living. It is hard to look back from today's perspectives at a different time when the current laws and regulations regarding drug use are in your mind and to understand that the early Mods taking amphetamines, were not doing anything illegal. Sometime around 1960 the amphetamine craze started in London's West End, and by 1963 it had become nationwide.

Mods used the drugs mainly for stimulation as well as for alertness. They viewed it as a different goal from intoxication or delirium caused by other drugs and alcohol. In fact, during those days, mod style and drug use is completely associated with one another. According to the Mods, cannabis was a substance that would slow a person down the exact opposite to what the youngsters were looking for. In those days Mods generally used amphetamines for extending their leisure time into the early hours of the morning and as a way of bridging the wide gap between their boring and often mundane everyday work lives and the weekend of dancing riding their scooters and dressing up on their weekends and living life to the full.

There is no doubting that the impact that amphetamines had on Mod culture was as significant as their fish tail parkas, scooters, fine clothing and the drudgery of the working week.

Following the well-publicised violence between Mods and Rockers in seaside resorts during 1964, newspapers reported on Mods emerging from clubs at 5am with dilated pupils and associating this with the violence that followed. This led to the criminalisation of their use by the government in July 1964.

After a new law came into force, the street price of Purple Hearts went up from 6d to 9d a tablet. It didn't make a lot of difference.

Purple Hearts (Drinamyl or [Dexamyl in the USA] made by Smith-Kline and French) were a combined amphetamine/barbiturate that was commonly prescribed to women for anxiety and as a dietary aid.

Durophet was another Mod favourite made by Riker and was coloured black and hence the name' Black Bombers'.

And that was it. Summer was over. Whilst Mods and Rockers spent the winter planning their tactics for 1965's Bank Holiday battles, so did the police: heavy tactics, even heavier fines. A general diluting of the original Mod spirit meant they were barely mentioned. And the fashion moved on,

new bands, new drugs and new styles. Me? I was a Southend on Sea Mod in 1963/64 and much of the story has basis in my own experiences of life during those heady days. Do I regret it......NO, and where did I end up living, Hastings for next thirty-five years!

The film 'Quadrophenia' was based on the real life Second Battle of Hastings in 1964 but was transposed to Brighton.

Printed in Great Britain
by Amazon